"I can assure you, Mark won't marry you."

"We'll just have to wait and see, won't we?" Ryan challenged, provoked by Grant's arrogance.

"Perhaps this will help your waiting!" Grant said, pulling her roughly against him to kiss her.

Ryan responded as if drugged before she pulled away with a gasp.

To her shame, Grant was looking down at her with cool emerald green eyes that were full of disgust. "Enough?" he drawled insultingly.

Ryan swallowed hard, her lips swollen with passion, realizing how easily she had succumbed to his lovemaking. "You're despicable!" she choked.

"I'm also Mark's brother. How do you think he'd feel about our lovemaking?"

She met his eyes with effort. "I'll ask him next time I speak to him," she returned coolly.

CAROLE MORTIMER
is also the author of these

Harlequin Presents

CAROLE MORTIMER

heaven here on earth

Harlequin Books

TORONTO • NEW YORK • LONDON
AMSTERDAM • PARIS • SYDNEY • HAMBURG
STOCKHOLM • ATHENS • TOKYO • MILAN

For
my mother-in-law,
Sylvia Mortimer

Harlequin Presents first edition August 1983
ISBN 0-373-10619-X

Original hardcover edition published in 1983
by Mills & Boon Limited

CHAPTER ONE

'YOU'LL love it there,' Mark assured her. 'I have the most fantastic studio.'

'Yes, but Yorkshire!' Ryan grimaced.

He frowned at her, a very good-looking man of twenty-four, with the overlong hair of their contemporaries, clear hazel-coloured eyes, dressed as casually as Ryan in denims and a loose-fitting shirt. 'I'll have you know Yorkshire is very beautiful at this time of year.'

'Beautiful Yorkshire in April!' she scorned, sitting opposite him in her flat while her flatmate Diana was in the bedroom preparing for her date with him. 'You just want to get rid of me for a few weeks so that you can pursue Diana without me in the way!'

Mark began to smile, his eyes crinkling at the corners, his teeth very white against his dark skin. 'How did you guess?'

'It wasn't hard!' She made a face.

He sat forward in his seat. 'Maybe my reasoning is partly selfish——'

'Mainly,' she substituted firmly.

'All right, mainly,' he sighed. 'But I really do have a great studio. My brother had the whole of the top floor of the house converted for me.'

'That's another thing—your family. How will they feel about having a complete stranger foisted on them?' Ryan frowned, looking younger than her twenty-one years with her long blonde hair and big blue eyes, her face small and heart-shaped. The deceptively youthful appearance hid a strong determination, a determination that had got her through art college against all the odds—that, as much as her talent, had won her a scholarship. It was at college that she had met Mark Montgomery, and while she had no romantic interest in him herself, he had been instantly attracted to her secretary friend and flatmate, Diana. The attraction was reluctantly reciprocated, as Diana doubted Mark's sincerity.

Ryan and Diana had been brought up in the children's home together, and both of them were a little wary of romantic relationships, although Diana more so, remembering her own parents and the bitter break-up of their marriage. In a way Ryan was a little luckier, she remembered nothing of her parents—if that could be called lucky!

Mark shrugged dismissively. 'They won't think anything of it, I often let friends use the studio. Besides, there's only Grant and Mandy, my brother and sister. Grant's always busy on the estate, and Mandy's only eighteen, so you'd be company for each other. And you don't have to stay in the main house, there's a cottage you can use on the estate.'

Ryan knew that Mark came from a wealthy family, that far from having to struggle through like a lot of their fellow-students, he always had plenty of money. The existence of the family estate in Yorkshire had come to light since he had been dating Diana, an incentive for her to trust him, Ryan believed. It had been wasted on Diana, just making her more wary.

'Besides,' he added enticingly, 'you don't want to pass up the opportunity of seeing a whole room full of Paul Gilbert paintings.'

Her eyes widened, the deep blue of violets, her lashes thick and silky, naturally dark. 'Your family

have a Paul Gilbert collection?' she gasped; Gilbert
was one of her favourite artists, and had been popular
for the last fifty years since his death.

'Better than that,' Mark said with satisfaction. 'He
was my great-grandfather. Encouragement enough?'

'If it's the truth,' Ryan said sceptically.

'Oh, it is,' he told her seriously.

She frowned. 'Then why haven't you mentioned
him before?'

He grinned, his eyes full of mischief. 'One doesn't
like to boast.'

'Doesn't one?' she taunted.

'No,' he shook his head. 'Especially when "one"
doesn't have even a tenth of his talent,' he added
seriously.

She raised dark blonde brows. 'Fishing for
compliments, Mark?' It was an accepted fact that
Mark had been the most talented one in the class
through the previous college year.

'No,' he laughed, dispelling the mood of seriousness.
'Oh, be a love, Ryan! Three weeks, three lovely weeks,
when you can have a studio all to yourself. You're
looking a little pale, the fresh air would put colour in
your cheeks——'

'All right, all right,' she interrupted laughingly, 'I'll
spend the Easter holidays in Yorkshire. But if you do
anything to hurt Diana while I'm away,' she sobered,
'I'll have you hanged, drawn, and quartered!
Understood?'

'Understood,' he nodded happily.

And so it was that two weeks later Ryan found
herself on a train bound for Yorkshire, her case in one
hand, her empty canvases in the other.

As the train neared the station for Sleaton her
trepidation grew. Mark swore he had made all the

arrangements, that he had told his family she would be arriving today, that his brother and sister didn't mind her visit in the least. But Mark wasn't known for his reliability. What if she should arrive at Montgomery Hall only to be turned away?

Montgomery Hall—just the name of it was enough to make her feel nervous, and it wasn't an emotion she usually admitted to. But Mark's family sounded a little out of her league, despite Mark's claim of how hard his brother worked on the estate, and how glad of her company Mandy would be.

Yes, Montgomery Hall sounded very daunting. And what would the Montgomerys make of Ryan Shelton?

She was wearing her newest denims, the ones with no paint splashed over them, and a light blue fluffy jumper that hugged her body and just touched the top of her denims, riding up a little if she should raise her arms. Despite it being April, and the sun shining brightly in a blue sky, there was a nip in the air, and although the jumper had shrunk a little in the wash, it was a pretty colour, and made her hair look like gold. It also emphasised the dark blue of her eyes.

The train drew slowly into the station of Sleaton, and she stepped down on to the platform, dragging her case off behind her, scratching it in the process. Not that it mattered, the case was battered enough already.

A couple of other people got off the train too, although they seemed surer of their destination, hurrying from the platform to disappear from the station building.

After dragging her case and canvases through the busy London station, with no chance of getting a porter, and Mark conveniently unavailable until the last minute, she had had no choice. But as the only person on this tiny station platform she should have been able to get help with her luggage now.

An old man leant on a broom a short distance away, bent over with age, looking as if he would fall down if someone were to remove the broom.

Ryan staggered over to him. 'Is there a porter?' she enquired politely.

'Yes,' he nodded, looking at her over the top of his gold-rimmed glasses, his hair and moustache a light grey colour.

She bit her tongue to stop her sharp retort. 'Could you tell me where he is, please?' She kept her voice light.

'I'm the porter, miss,' he told her in an important voice, as if daring her to challenge his claim.

She wouldn't dare! 'Would you mind carrying my case?' she persisted brightly.

He looked down at the battered brown case at her feet. 'It looks on the heavy side.'

'It is,' she nodded.

'I've got a bad back, you know,' he began to shake his head. 'The doctor told me to lay off heavy lifting.'

Again Ryan bit her tongue, deciding silence would be better than any criticism she would care to make about a porter who couldn't lift heavy objects. By the look of Sleaton it was a small community, and this man could be related to half the population! Upsetting the village people would be a great start with the Montgomery family.

She gave a resigned shrug and moved to the lady taking the tickets. She looked as if she could be the porter's wife!

'You mustn't mind Jack,' the woman confided. 'He retires next month.'

Not before time, by the look of him! And that didn't exactly help her now. She could see she would have to become used to a slower and less efficient way of life the next few weeks.

Still, as Mark had claimed, Yorkshire was looking very beautiful; the gorse was in full bloom, everywhere a deep rich green after the early April showers. Flowers were in bloom along the neat garden at the side of the station—although Ryan doubted if Jack kept it in that neat state. Too much bending!

She thought of the next three weeks, three weeks of peace and quiet, three weeks of sketching and painting as much as she wanted to. Heaven on earth!

Once she got outside the station she looked around for possible transport to Montgomery Hall. There wasn't any! She doubted this sleepy little village, with its homes all grey-brick thatched cottages, sported a local taxi. And Mark didn't seem to have taken into account the fact that she had to get from the station to the house. The idea of a holiday in this remote part of Yorkshire suddenly began to lose its magic, the white-painted cottage that had the look of a picture-postcard beauty seeming perhaps too much of a drastic change from London. Well, it was too late to change her mind now!

She went back to the ticket-collector, who also seemed to double as the ticket-seller!

'Going straight back, are you, love?' she quipped. 'The shortest stay on record,' she smiled at her own joke. 'We usually keep our visitors a little longer.'

Ryan smiled back, beginning to feel weary now. 'I was wondering if there's a local taxi . . .?' She hardly dared voice the question.

The woman frowned. 'Bert Jenkins from the village used to do a bit of driving, but he's got a funny leg.'

'Funny leg . . .?' Ryan returned resignedly, beginning to think the whole village had one medical complaint or another.

'Arthritis, I think,' the woman nodded.

'So there's no taxi?'

'Not any more.' The woman shook her head.

Ryan pursed her lips and straightened her shoulders determinedly. 'In that case, could you direct me to Montgomery Hall?'

The woman's interest deepened. 'Friend of the family, are you?'

'Er—yes.' She was taken aback at this open questioning, being used to the surliness of London transport workers.

'Would you be the friend of Mr Mark's they're expecting?'

Her eyes widened even more. 'Er—yes, I would. How did you know?'

The woman laughed. 'Not much is a secret in Sleaton! Besides, my sister-in-law helps out in the house.'

'I see,' Ryan nodded. 'The directions?' she prompted.

'Oh—of course.' The woman looked disappointed that she didn't want to stay and chat. 'Turn right out of the station, it's about three miles down that road——'

'*Three miles?*'

'Mm,' the woman nodded. 'You can't miss it. A big old manor house on the right-hand side of the road, set behind high iron gates.'

Ryan thanked the woman and moved off a little way down the road. *Three miles!* She couldn't remember the last time she had walked that far—and certainly not with a heavy case and half a dozen canvases.

It looked a very long winding road, with a stone wall either side, the same grey stone the cottages and farmhouses were built from, and she began to see several of the latter as she walked along, the occasional dog barking in the distance, lambs bleating to their mothers in the fields. Ryan had never seen so many sheep in her life, they seemed to be everywhere, and most of the ewes were accompanied by one or two young frisky lambs. Spring was a beautiful time, a time of new beginnings, when all the world seemed fresh and new. Maybe it would be a new beginning for her too?

It was over a month since she and Alan had decided they weren't suited, and yet she still hadn't been able to accept the fact that he was gone from her life. Her break-up with him was partly the reason she had been so easy to persuade to come here, although after the first mile or so she was beginning to more than regret the decision. With no obvious public transport and no car of her own, she was going to be very tied to Montgomery Hall for the duration of her stay here.

In that moment she forgot all about how tired she was, and how much her legs ached, as a huge dog suddenly bounded down the road towards her! It looked enormous, a dirty grey and white colour, and Ryan looked around desperately for somewhere to hide. There wasn't anywhere, and she held her case and canvases protectively in front of her. So much for the pleasure of the countryside; she was going to be attacked by a wild dog now!

But instead of attacking her the dog put its front paws on her thighs, looking up at her expectantly, its tongue hanging out, its stumpy tail wagging in a friendly manner.

'Why, you're just a big softie!' Ryan went down on her haunches beside the dog, roughly patting its neck. He didn't have a collar on, she ascertained that much.

She also realised that his fur was all matted, besides being dirty, as if he hadn't had a good brush in weeks. In fact he looked neglected altogether. 'Where's your owner, boy?' She looked about them for an angry farmer demanding she leave his dog alone, but all she saw were the inevitable sheep in the neighbouring fields. 'Are you lost then, hmm?' she allowed the dog to jump over her excitedly. 'I think you are,' she nodded, standing up to brush down her denims, the dog's dirty paws having put dusty marks all over them. 'Maybe we'll find him on the way,' she reassured the bright-eyed animal as he gazed up at her adoringly. 'You walk along with me. I could do with the company anyway,' she added ruefully.

The dog needed no second bidding, but trotted along happily at her heels. Just having him along with her lightened her own mood, the sun suddenly seemed brighter, the birds sang happily in the trees.

She glanced down at the dog occasionally, realising that underneath all that dust he was probably an Old English Sheepdog. It seemed a shame that someone had let him get into this state. A good wash and brush-up and he would be a beautiful dog. And he had a lovely friendly nature, occasionally running off to chase an unsuspecting butterfly, coming back to her side quite happily once the creature flew out of his reach.

He was still at her side when a Land Rover appeared on the road behind her, the first vehicle to pass down the road either way.

'Careful, Ragtag,' she soothed as the dog began to growl at the approaching vehicle. 'Mm, it suits you,' she said ruefully as she realised the name she had unwittingly given him. 'Now behave,' she warned. 'And if we're lucky we may get a lift the rest of the way. I'm already beginning to fear for my sanity—this is the first time I've had a conversation with a dog!'

The Land Rover went straight past her, giving her a brief glimpse of the man behind the wheel, the peaked cap he wore concealing his face. The vehicle suddenly came to a halt a few yards past her.

She ran eagerly to the passenger side, and the man in the driving-seat leaned over to wind down the window.

'Like a lift?' he offered; he was a man probably in his early thirties, with hair as blond as her own, with warm blue eyes, very attractive in an outdoor sort of way. 'Don't worry,' he smiled at her hesitation, 'I'm the local vet, so if I attacked you the whole area would know about it in ten minutes!'

She laughed, instantly liking him. 'I'm going to Montgomery Hall——'

'Mark's friend,' he nodded, already climbing out from behind the wheel.

Ryan followed him to the back of the vehicle, watching as he opened the double doors. 'Does everyone in Sleaton know I'm coming here?' she asked with a sigh, handing him her suitcase. 'No, I'll keep the canvases,' she clung to them.

He smiled. 'Okay. And the answer to your question is yes. There isn't much that's a secret in a place this size. I'm surprised Grant didn't send someone to pick you up,' he frowned.

Ryan grimaced. 'Well, I thought that was because Mark had forgotten to tell them that I was coming, but that's been firmly ruled out.'

'Not necessarily,' he shook his head. 'He could have forgotten to tell them *when* you were arriving.'

'That sounds like Mark,' she nodded.

'Yes,' the young vet laughed. 'My name's Peter Thornby, by the way.'

'Ryan Shelton,' she introduced herself.

'Nice to meet you,' he shook her hand. 'Where's your dog gone? I thought he could go in the back with your suitcase, I have a wire mesh up.'

Ryan looked down in surprise. Ragtag seemed to have disappeared! She frowned, looking up and down the road. He had gone. She felt strangely alone again.

'He wasn't my dog actually,' she explained huskily, already missing him. She had never had a dog make friends with her before, and the liking had been mutual. 'He just followed me. You haven't seen him before?' As the local vet he might have come across Ragtag in his work.

Peter Thornby shook his head. 'I didn't get a good look at him, but I don't think I've had him as a patient. Still, that isn't surprising, he could be living wild. He didn't look very old.'

Ryan climbed into the Land Rover beside him, still looking out of the side-window for Ragtag. He couldn't have disappeared so completely. It was pretty open countryside, with a few odd trees, masses and masses of gorse bushes, an occasional wall to divide the fields, certainly nowhere a dog of Ragtag's size could really hide. And yet he had gone.

Peter Thornby started up the engine. 'I shouldn't worry about it, Ryan. He could turn up again, but then again, he's survived this long on his own, there's no reason why he shouldn't continue to do so.'

She knew he was right, and yet she couldn't help missing the friendly dog. She hoped that, as Peter Thornby said, he would continue to be able to take care of himself.

She shook off her despondency with effort and turned to look at the man at her side. He was dressed in a dark green anorak and old brown corduroys, his feet thrust into wellington boots, the bottoms of his trousers tucked inside them.

'Do you live locally?' Ryan asked conversationally.

'About five miles away.' He drove the large vehicle confidently down the narrow lane. 'I have a large area to cover,' he smiled.

'Is it far to Montgomery Hall?'

'About another half mile. Why didn't you call Grant from the station?' he frowned. 'I'm sure he would have sent a car for you.'

Ryan grimaced. 'I don't even know him, I thought it seemed a bit of a cheek. I tried to get a taxi, but——'

'Bert's leg is playing him up.'

Her eyes widened. 'How did you know?'

Peter spluttered with laughter. 'He's used the same excuse for the last twenty years.'

She smiled too. 'How does he make a living?'

Peter shrugged. 'I have no idea, but he manages somehow. And if he gets a bit short of cash his leg is miraculously better for a couple of weeks. Once you've been in Sleaton a few days you'll realise it's full of characters like Bert Jenkins.'

'And Jack the porter,' she joined in his teasing.

'Right,' he nodded with a grin. 'He's got a bad back, you know,' he told her in a derisive voice.

'So have I now!'

'How do you like Sleaton so far?' he quirked a mocking eyebrow.

Ryan gave a laugh of enjoyment. 'Strangely enough, very much.'

'Me too. I even came back here after completing my training.' He brought the Land Rover to a halt and turned with his arm along the back of her seat. 'Well, here we are.'

'We are?' She looked over to the right-hand side of

the road. Montgomery Hall was indeed behind 'huge iron gates', as the woman at the station had told her; it was also surrounded by a ten-foot wall!

She couldn't help her gasp of surprise, as her gaze passed on to the house itself, a big Georgian manor house about half a mile from the gate down a gravel driveway, neatly laid lawns and trees fronting the house, with a gardener busy working on the numerous flower-beds.

Peter was watching her reaction. 'Impressive, isn't it?'

What an understatement! 'Very,' she gulped.

'It's just as beautiful inside,' he told her. 'I wish I had the time to drive you down to the house, but I was called out to a sick cow over half an hour ago . . .'

'You've been very kind already.' Ryan got down from the Land Rover and came round to get her case from the back. 'Thank you,' she smiled up at him.

He nodded. 'My pleasure. No doubt I'll see you again soon. And if you do happen to see that dog again perhaps you could bring him to my surgery? I usually call in at Sleaton Monday and Friday evenings.'

She frowned. 'You don't think there's anything wrong with him?'

'Not at all,' he answered instantly. 'But I doubt if it would do any harm to have him examined.'

'I'll bring him if I see him.' She somehow felt a responsibility to the stray dog.

'Fine,' he smiled. 'Give my regards to Grant and Mandy.'

Ryan turned to look at the house once again when Peter had driven off. She had been right to suppose it was a big house, only it was all more, much more, than she had imagined. She only hoped Mandy and Grant Montgomery proved to be as nice as Mark.

She felt something wet nuzzling her hand, and looked down to see Ragtag. Her face lit up with pleasure, and she bent down to him. 'Where did you go?' She cuddled him, regardless of his dirty coat. 'I thought you'd gone for good! But I'm glad you haven't—I was beginning to feel like Maria in *The Sound of Music*, standing out here looking up at the house. Still,' she stood up, 'at least there aren't seven children in there—I hope!' she grimaced.

It took all her strength to open the gate, and she made no objection when the dog followed her. She liked his company. Besides, he gave her confidence.

The gardener gave her a curious look as she walked down the driveway, and she suddenly realised what a mess she must look. She was covered in dust from cuddling Ragtag, her hair was windswept, and her case even more disreputable after being in the back of Peter Thornby's Land Rover. It looked as if he often carried animals in there. She shrugged resignedly; there was nothing she could do about her appearance now.

'You'll have to stay outside,' she instructed the dog as she rang the doorbell. 'I just have to pick up the key to the cottage. I think one Ragtag going inside is enough,' she added ruefully.

The butler didn't even blink an eyelid when she told him who she was. 'Miss Amanda is in the drawing-room,' he told her stiffly.

Thank goodness she was staying in a cottage on the estate—far away from the main house, she hoped. She was used to doing what she wanted, when she wanted. It must be strange having a houseful of servants.

'Stay, Ragtag,' she instructed as he sat down on the top step. 'I shouldn't be long,' she added hopefully, leaving her luggage in the hallway before following the butler through to the drawing-room. At least she was going to meet the Montgomerys one at a time!

It was a very long room, almost running the entire length of the house, and the whole room had an air of comfortable elegance; one end was obviously the sitting area, the suite having an unobtrusive floral pattern, the curtains at the long windows matching the pattern exactly.

Huge double doors were opened into the garden at the other end of the informal room, and it was the girl seated behind the piano who held Ryan's attention. She couldn't be any other than Mark's sister; she had his rich dark hair, kept short and boyish, her eyes, as she stared sightlessly into the garden, were the same hazel colour. She was a pretty girl, extremely so, and her pale lilac dress suited her dark colouring.

The butler coughed rather pointedly, and although the girl's shoulders stiffened slightly she made no effort to stop playing, her fingers flowing fluidly over the piano keys. Ryan had no sense of music, modern or old, but she thought this playing was probably good.

Suddenly the girl crashed all ten fingers down on to the keys and turned to face them, her eyes flashing. 'What is it, Shelley?' she snapped in a haughty voice, totally ignoring Ryan as she stood beside him.

The butler appeared unperturbed by her abruptness. 'Miss Ryan Shelton,' he announced.

Cool hazel eyes were turned on Ryan, who withstood the appraisal very well in the circumstances. This girl was very insolent, nothing at all like the easygoing Mark.

'Thank you, Shelley,' she said dismissively, not even looking at him. 'You may go.' She stood up, a tall girl; her lilac dress was very elegantly styled, her legs long and shapely, the heels high on her matching sandals. 'So you're Ryan Shelton,' she mused slowly. 'My brother's little friend from college.'

Ryan bit her lip, not taking to Amanda Montgomery at all. She only hoped first impressions were wrong! 'Mark and I are at college together, yes,' she answered calmly, feeling her untidiness more against this young girl's sophistication. She looked much older than the eighteen Mark had said she was! As for the two of them being company for each other—the only thing they had in common was their youth!

'My name's Mandy.' The other girl began to thaw a little, humour lightening her eyes. 'You aren't what Grant was expecting at all,' she commented.

'No?' Ryan frowned.

'No. You see, he——' Mandy broke off as a man strode into the room, a man who instantly held Ryan's attention.

He had to be Grant Montgomery, that much was obvious once again by his dark colouring, but that was where all similarity to Mark ended! This man was incredibly tall, well over six feet, with the powerful physique of an athlete, his shoulders wide, a flat hardened stomach, muscular thighs and long legs all shown to advantage in the checked working shirt and close-fitting faded denims.

But it was his face that held her attention. It wasn't just that he was so much older than she had expected, at least ten years Mark's senior, it was also that he was so incredibly good-looking, in a harsh way. His hair grew long and dark over his ears and collar, his face was tanned a dark teak colour from the wind and sunshine he worked in, his eyes were the colour of emeralds, the nose long and hawkish, the top lip of the firmly compressed mouth thin and uncompromising, the lower lip fuller, sensually so. His jaw was firm and strong, the top two buttons of his shirt were unbuttoned to reveal an equally tanned chest.

Those green eyes flickered over her with a keen intelligence, his brows lifting slightly in surprise. 'I didn't know you had a friend coming over this afternoon, Mandy.' His voice was deep and gravelly, sending shivers of awareness down Ryan's spine.

His sister's mouth twisted. 'I haven't.'

The green eyes narrowed now. 'Then who——'

'Ryan Shelton,' Mandy supplied with obvious relish.

He drew in an angry breath. 'Another of Mark's little jokes, I take it?' he rasped, his voice no longer pleasurable to listen to in his displeasure.

Ryan listened to the exchange between brother and sister with a sinking heart. It didn't sound as if she was exactly welcome here! And Mark had sworn he had arranged everything! She should have known. She would kill him when she got back to——

'Please excuse us, Miss Shelton,' Grant Montgomery spoke to her directly now. 'When Mark informed us of your visit he omitted one thing.'

At least it was only one!

'The fact that you're a girl,' Grant finished in a derisive voice.

Ryan swallowed hard, as the sinking feeling returned. 'He did?' she grimaced. What did it mean? Wasn't she welcome if she was a girl?

'Yes,' Grant Montgomery bit out, his eyes icy now, derogative as he looked her up and down. 'He merely said it would be a friend called Ryan.'

'Does it make a difference?' She chewed on her bottom lip.

'To your visit here? No,' he shrugged dismissively. 'Although I'm a little surprised at your interest in art.'

'Interest?' she echoed sharply. 'It's more than an interest, it's my career,' she defended, sensing his criticism.

'Oh yes?' he scorned. 'And what do you intend doing with it?'

'Well, I——'

'Because unless you have an exceptional talent,' which his tone seemed to imply he doubted, 'or intend going into advertising or teaching, art is a complete waste of time, especially for a woman.'

Ryan flushed. 'Maybe I have an exceptional talent,' she snapped, her chin at a challenging angle.

'Maybe,' Grant Montgomery drawled. 'And now you have the use of an exceptional studio. But not of the cottage, I'm afraid,' he added with a frown.

'No?' She tried to remain calm in the face of what looked like being a wasted journey. Even supposing Grant Montgomery did let her have the use of the studio, she doubted if the village had a hotel. If it didn't have a taxi it was highly unlikely to have a hotel!

'No. You see——' He broke off as a strange noise sounded through the house. 'What the hell——!' He strode off through the open patio doors to the back of the house where the noise appeared to be coming from.

Ryan followed more slowly. She already knew what the strange noise was. Ragtag howling. . . .

CHAPTER TWO

HE was still howling when the three of them reached the back of the house, sitting in the cobbled yard with his head raised to the clear blue sky, howling soulfully, as if his very life depended on it.

Grant Montgomery came to an abrupt halt, staring incredulously at the scruffy dog. 'Good grief,' he blinked, as if his eyes had to be deceiving him. 'What on earth is *that*?'

Ryan bridled at his scornful tone, and Ragtag stopped his howling long enough to growl at the tall imposing man who looked down at him so disdainfully.

'It looks like a dog,' said Mandy in amusement.

'It is a dog!' Ryan moved to Ragtag's side, going down on her haunches to have her face licked ecstatically by her new canine friend. She glared up at the brother and sister. '*My* dog,' she told them angrily.

Grant's brows rose arrogantly. 'You're expecting him to stay here too?'

'You said I couldn't use the cottage,' she reminded him, standing up, but keeping the now quiet Ragtag at her side.

'At this moment, unfortunately not. Some of the roof tiles have come loose during the winter storms, something that wasn't discovered until yesterday when the cottage was opened up for you. I have a man working on it now, but until such time as the repairs are completed and the cottage is aired for you you're welcome to stay in the house.' He looked down at Ragtag. 'The dog is not.'

She looked down at Ragtag too, seeing what Grant Montgomery must see, a dirty unbrushed mutt, desperately in need of a good cleaning. But she also saw the trust in his deep brown eyes as he watched her, the almost stupidly loving expression on his face, his tail wagging goodnaturedly. If what Peter Thornby said was truth, that Ragtag was probably a stray, then there was no reason why he shouldn't become her dog.

'I have two dogs of my own,' Grant Montgomery added before she could make any comment. 'Two Golden Labradors. I doubt they would welcome——' he paused pointedly.

'Ragtag,' she mumbled at his prompting.

'How appropriate,' Mandy taunted.

Ryan flashed her a look of dislike. 'That's what I thought.'

'Yes, well,' Grant Montgomery's mouth showed signs of a smile, although it never materialised, 'Rex and Riba don't like strange dogs in their home. But that isn't to say your dog isn't welcome to stay, as you are,' this last seemed to come out rather grudgingly. 'Would you mind if he slept in the stable until the cottage is ready? It will only be for a couple of nights.'

Considering Ragtag was probably used to sleeping under the stars, a stable would probably be a luxury to him. And yet Ryan was aware that Grant Montgomery was only making a token show of seeking her approval, that it was the stable or nothing. Her mutt mustn't be allowed to mix with his purebred Labradors!

'I realise he needs a bath——'

'That's an understatement,' Mandy mocked.

Again Ryan looked at her with dislike. Snobbish

little cat! 'We happen to have travelled a long way,' she flashed. 'Both of us got rather dusty on the walk from the station.'

'You *walked*?' the other girl gasped.

She stiffened. 'Of course.'

Grant Montgomery was frowning, the problem of Ragtag forgotten. 'You came by train?'

'Why else would I be at the station?'

His eyes hardened as he met the anger in hers. 'Mark didn't tell us you would be coming by train.'

'Does it matter?' she dismissed, becoming more and more disenchanted with this situation.

'Not at all,' he answered coldly. 'Except there was no need for you to have walked all that way. A telephone call and one of us would have come and got you.'

She shrugged. 'I managed to get a lift in the end.'

'Oh yes?'

Ryan sensed his disapproval. However, she was twenty-one, not twelve, and she certainly didn't have to ask this man's permission to accept the offer of a lift! She didn't relish the thought of being a guest in his home for the next few days either. Staying in a cottage on the estate was one thing, living in the house, if only for a couple of days, was something else completely. It meant she would be thrown into close daily contact with both Grant and Mandy Montgomery. And what she had seen of them so far didn't endear them to her.

'With the vet,' she told them casually. 'A very nice man. He sent his regards.'

'So you've met Peter,' Mandy said slowly.

Ryan looked at her curiously, sensing a deep interest behind the casual question. The other girl had a delicate flush to her cheeks, a glow to her eyes. Could it be that she was more than a little interested in the local vet? If she were it was obvious from Grant Montgomery's haughty expression that he knew nothing about it. Would he approve or not? Peter Thornby was a lot older than Mandy, but then the girl was headstrong, maybe maturity was what she needed.

She firmly dismissed the other girl's interest from her mind. It was none of her business who Mandy—or Grant, for that matter—fell in love with. She was just here to paint, and the sooner she could move into that cottage the better it would be as far as she was concerned.

'Yes, I met him,' she nodded. 'He was in a hurry, though, so he couldn't stop.'

Mandy's mouth tightened angrily. 'He never can!' She turned on her heel and walked back into the house.

More than interested, Ryan would say. An unreturned interest, by the look of it.

Grant Montgomery looked taken aback by his sister's behaviour, an emotion he quickly masked as he turned back to Ryan. 'I'll show you where the dog can sleep,' he said abruptly, leading the way over to the stables.

She slowly followed him, aware of the power he exuded, his strides long and purposeful, muscles rippling beneath his shirt as he swung the door open.

'One of the stalls should be all right,' he told her.

Ryan had the feeling he would like to allocate her to one of the stalls too! It really hadn't been a good idea to come here, it wasn't working out at all as she had expected. So far there had been none of the peace and quiet she wanted.

'Yes, fine,' she agreed dully, the stable pristine clean.

Grant Montgomery looked down at her. 'If you would rather he came up to the house——'

'No, it doesn't matter,' she dismissed curtly. 'I think he needs a bath first—like me,' she added ruefully, blatantly aware that even though Grant Montgomery had supposedly been working on the estate all day he was much tidier than she was, and the heated smell of his body was rather pleasant to the senses. Potent, was a much more appropriate word.

He really was an attractive man, magnetically so, somewhere in his mid-thirties, she would have guessed. Mark had told her that his brother wasn't married, and now, having met him, she found that surprising. Some lucky woman should have snapped him up long ago, maybe then he wouldn't have adopted this arrogant air of condescension. Although she wouldn't have counted on it! He had the look of a man who had always had supreme self-confidence.

He nodded now, not disclaiming her comment. 'I'll get Shelley to show you to your room. You can get some food for your dog in the kitchen once you've freshened up.'

Ryan was relieved he had mentioned that. She had been wondering what to do about feeding Ragtag, especially as it already seemed she had to accept the Montgomerys' hospitality for herself for several days.

'Thank you,' she accepted.

'Perhaps you would like to settle the dog and then come up to the house,' Grant suggested distantly. 'I have to get back to work, but Shelley will be only too happy to help you should you run into any difficulties.'

'Er——fine,' she said. 'I-I'll see you later, then.'

'At dinner,' he nodded tersely.

Ryan's last view of him was as he strode off to climb in behind the wheel of his Land Rover, a grey one this time, as opposed to Peter Thornby's green one, then

Grant Montgomery drove off towards the fields at the back of the house. Considering the amount of sheep she had seen on her way here it was natural to assume the estate farmed them.

Mark hadn't really told her much about his family, least of all their complexities. Mandy was a strange girl, old beyond her years in some ways, still very young in others, and Grant Montgomery was too full of complexities to even begin to fathom him. And she would bet that a lot of women had tried.

'Interesting man,' she told Ragtag as she looked for a comfortable spot for him in one of the stalls. 'Oh, I know you didn't like him,' she smiled, 'but then he didn't seem too keen on you either. Ah, here we are,' she had found a stall full of fresh-smelling hay. 'Now you settle down here,' she instructed. 'And I'll bring you some food down soon. And just between you and me, Ragtag,' she said in a whisper, 'I don't think the haughty Mr Grant Montgomery liked me either!'

It had been there from the beginning, an antagonism that was not of her making, almost as if he suspected her motives for being here. Oh, how she wished that cottage had been ready for her when she arrived, or that she had known of the delay and could have come a couple of days later. In the meantime she would have to make the best of it.

'I'll be back soon,' she absently assured the dog, and went back into the house to seek out the butler.

The bedroom they had given her was as elegantly furnished as the rest of the house, the carpet cream and fluffy, the deep pink bedspread and velvet curtains at the windows matching perfectly, the furniture a light pine.

Her suitcase had already been placed on the ottoman at the bottom of the double bed, with her canvases propped against it, reminding her of her reason for being here. Tomorrow she would be able to start work, that would compensate for all the difficulties she had so far encountered.

She was just putting on her clean clothing after her bath when Mandy Montgomery walked into the room unnanounced. Ryan hastily straightened her tee-shirt over her breasts, smoothing it over her denims. If Mandy had hoped to unnerve her she had failed. After sharing a dormitory with five other girls, Diana being one of them, she had become used to a lack of privacy, and was completely lacking in inhibitions about her body.

Nevertheless, she faced the other girl challengingly, knowing the intrusion had been a deliberately rude one. 'Yes?' she enquired coolly.

'You're wanted on the telephone——'

'Mark?' Her expression brightened, and she forgot her antagonism.

'Of course,' Mandy taunted. 'You can use the telephone in the drawing-room.'

Ryan didn't wait to hear any more, but ran down the stairs to pick up the telephone. 'Mark!' she greeted him with breathless relief.

'Who else?' he said cheerfully. 'How's it going?'

'Well, I had to walk from the station, the house is *enormous*, my cottage isn't ready, I have——'

'Hey, slow down, slow down!' he laughed. 'I heard all about that from Mandy. I also heard you had some strange-looking animal with you. I'm sure you were alone when Diana and I saw you off this morning,' he teased.

Mandy hadn't wasted much time relating her unusual arrival. 'You almost saw me off,' she reminded him. 'You arrived just as the train was pulling out of the station. As for the dog, he's adopted me,' she dismissed. 'Mark, your brother has very kindly invited me to stay in the house until the cottage is ready, but——'

'Have you seen the studio yet?' he interrupted.

She frowned. 'No.'

'Get Mandy to show it to you. I guarantee you won't want to leave then.'

'I don't *want* to leave now. I just feel—uncomfortable, with your family.' That was the understatement of the year!

'What did you think of Grant?'

'Think of him?' she returned guardedly.

Mark chuckled softly. 'Handsome devil, isn't he?'

'Very handsome,' she acknowledged stiffly.

'I thought you'd like him,' he mocked.

'Who said anything about liking him?' she snapped, knowing that she was, foolishly, blushing. 'I just admitted he was handsome, that doesn't mean I like him.'

'Of course not,' Mark replied blandly. 'And how about Mandy, what do you think of her?'

'She's very pretty.'

'Isn't she?' The smile could be heard in his voice as he guessed at her evasion. 'She's also very sweet under the bitchiness.'

'I'm not sure I'll get that far,' Ryan said dryly.

'You will,' he laughed. 'Could you put her on for a few minutes? I want to talk to her.'

Much to Ryan's embarrassment she found Mandy Montgomery standing in the open doorway when she turned, giving every impression of having been there for some time. How much of the conversation had she listened to? She hoped not the part where she had admitted that Grant was handsome!

'He wants to talk to you,' she held out the receiver to the other girl.

Mandy strolled over, in no hurry. 'Thanks,' and she instantly turned her back on Ryan.

So much for getting past the bitchiness! She wasn't even sure she wanted to.

'I'm not your servant!' Mandy was telling her brother angrily. 'All right,' she agreed finally. 'But Grant isn't too happy about the way you deceived him. You know exactly what I mean. It isn't funny, Mark, Grant is furious about it.'

It didn't need two guesses what Grant Montgomery was 'furious' about. He had been expecting a man, and instead she had turned up. She was always having the same trouble with her name, although this time she was inclined to believe, as Grant did, that Mark had done it on purpose. It was the sort of thing he would find funny. Obviously his brother didn't share his sense of humour. She wasn't sure she did in this case either. It had certainly got her off to a bad start with the other two members of the Montgomery family.

Mandy had rung off now, and turned to her with that insolent stare. 'Mark wants me to show you the studio.'

She blushed. 'If you'd rather not, I'm sure I could find it on my own.'

Dark eyebrows rose in a facsimile of her eldest brother. 'I doubt if Grant would welcome you wandering about the house on your own,' she drawled.

Ryan's mouth tightened at the other girl's insulting tone. 'I don't think your family silver would look right in my flat,' she snapped.

Mandy smiled, at once looking younger. 'So you can stand up for yourself if you have to. That could come in useful in this house.' She led the way up the stairs, with Ryan walking at her side. 'Don't be fooled by Grant's mild manner of earlier, he can be a swine at times.'

If his rudeness to her and condescension to Ragtag had been his mild manner, then he must indeed be a swine at his worst! 'I'll remember that,' she said coolly.

'I should,' Mandy advised softly. 'When Grant has one of his boils the whole household knows about it.'

'Then let's hope that he doesn't "boil" while I'm in the house!'

'I wouldn't count on it,' the other girl said dryly. 'It happens pretty regularly. Here's the studio,' she flung open double doors at the top of the last flight of stairs, standing aside for Ryan to enter.

As Ryan walked inside she forgot all about Mandy's snobbishness, Grant's arrogance, Mark's disregard for anything but his own plans, and her face lit up as she took in the perfection of the studio. Mark certainly hadn't exaggerated.

The studio covered most of the loft space, huge windows having been put in as skylights each side of the sloping roof, giving the room a very light and airy feeling. Several easels stood about the room, empty of canvases, in fact, the whole room had an unused look.

'Mark doesn't use it very often,' Mandy stated the obvious. 'He doesn't come home very often either,' she added in a resentful voice. 'He prefers his London friends.'

'Really?' Ryan was only half listening, her excitement increasing as she looked around the room. It was perfect, absolutely perfect. She could spend the rest of her life working in here. Although three weeks would have to do!

'Are you a—special friend of his?' Mandy probed.

She shrugged. 'I don't know about special, but I've known him a long time.' She was already planning where she would put her easel for the best light. How her fellow students would envy her this opportunity, most of them having to make do, as she usually did. She had a feeling she was going to do some of her best work here.

'If you've quite finished looking round,' Mandy said tightly.

'Mm? Oh—oh yes,' Ryan blushed. 'It's lovely,' she said inadequately.

The other girl nodded. 'Mark often lets his friends use it, but you're the first female.'

This fact really seemed to bother the Montgomery family, although Ryan couldn't for the life of her think why. Didn't they have friends of both sexes?

'Perhaps you would like to join me for tea in the lounge?' Mandy asked grudgingly.

'I'd like that,' she accepted. 'But I have to feed my dog first.'

The other girl's mouth twisted mockingly. 'I'll see you later, then.'

So dismissed, Ryan made her way down to the kitchen, finding that Grant had already told the cook she would be requiring the food.

Ragtag sat outside the stable rather than inside it, basking in the sunshine, although he got up and trotted to her side as soon as he saw her, his nose going into the food-bowl as if he hadn't eaten for a month.

'Take it easy!' she laughed, as more food seemed to come over the side of the bowl rather than into his mouth, the water slopping out of the other bowl as he almost leapt inside it. Ragtag carried on eating until all the food had gone, looking up at her expectantly once the bowl was empty. 'More!' Ryan chided, standing up. 'I bet Grant will be glad to get rid of us, Ragtag.' She frowned down at him. 'Maybe once you've had a bath you won't look so ragtaggled.'

'Talking to yourself could become a dangerous habit,' a familiar gravelly voice taunted her.

She blushed, looking up at Grant Montgomery, finding it impossible to read his expression, as the sun was directly behind him. For such a big man he moved very quietly, she hadn't even been aware of his presence in the cobbled yard until he spoke.

'Talking to a dog could be an even more dangerous one,' she returned softly, shushing the ungrateful Ragtag as he began to growl at the intruder.

'You think so?' Grant mocked.

'I'm hoping not,' she said ruefully. 'I seem to be doing it all the time.'

'I believe when the dog answers you is the time to begin worrying,' he drawled dryly. 'Are you joining us for tea?' he briskly changed the subject.

It was as well that he had; Ryan was open-mouthed about his show of humour. It came as something of a surprise after his earlier rudeness, and was totally in opposition to his harsh expression as he moved out of the sun.

'I—I'll just go and wash first,' she mumbled.

'Very well,' he nodded abruptly, as if regretting the softening of his mood, striding off into the house.

Ryan went up to her room to wash, then hurried down to the drawing-room to join the brother and sister for tea. She was beginning to feel rather hungry, a sandwich or two would see her through until it was time for dinner.

'It's all right for you,' Mandy was complaining when Ryan reached the drawing-room door. 'You're out at work most of the day, but how am I supposed to entertain this friend of Mark's?'

Ryan's hand froze in the action of opening the door. They were talking about her!

'She doesn't need entertaining,' Grant dismissed. 'Just leave her to her scribbles up in the studio.'

Scribbles! Ryan could feel her temper beginning to rise. How dared he call her work 'scribbles'!

'After all, it is partly Mark's home too—even if he does rarely use it,' Grant added hardly. 'If he wants this girl to stay here as his guest then he has a perfect right to expect us to let her. It's only for three weeks, Mandy,' he consoled. 'Then we'll probably never see her again.'

'I wouldn't be too sure of that.' The scowl could be heard in his sister's voice. 'Mark called her earlier, and they seemed very friendly.'

'If it lasts as long as Mark's other "friendships" I won't worry too much,' Grant derided.

'She also thinks you're handsome,' Mandy mused. 'I wonder what Valerie would think of that.'

'She wouldn't think anything,' Grant snapped. 'The opinion of one of Mark's Bohemian girl-friends is not in the least important to either Valerie or myself.'

Ryan didn't want to listen to any more; she ran back to her bedroom before her presence outside the door was detected, leaning back against the door once she was safely inside her room.

How dared he! Bohemian girl-friend, indeed! No wonder Mark rarely came here if that was the sort of opinion he had to put up with. And Mandy—how could she have repeated that remark she had made about Grant being handsome!

How was she supposed to face him again after that? And who was Valerie? Mark hadn't mentioned his brother having a girl-friend, but in the circumstances she could not think who else Valerie could be.

She couldn't go down there now, not after what she had just heard, it would be too embarrassing.

'Miss Shelton?' A knock sounded on the door to accompany the butler's query.

She swallowed hard, straightening her hair before opening the door to him. 'Yes?' She sounded cool enough.

'Mr Montgomery asked me to enquire if you had changed your mind about joining them for tea?'

'Er—yes,' she said jerkily. 'I—I have a bit of a headache, I thought I'd go for a walk instead.' Her voice gained confidence as her excuse took shape. 'Please give them my apologies.'

'Of course, miss,' the middle-aged man nodded. 'Is there anything I can get you? Aspirin?'

'The fresh air is all I need,' she smiled brightly. 'Thank you.'

She picked up her jacket once he had gone, then hurried from the house, collecting Ragtag to set off across the fields at the back of the house. There were sheep everywhere, most of the ewes having a young lamb gambolling at their side.

It was the latter that finally calmed her, and she sat on a wall to watch their antics, finding the little twins the funniest, each trying for a place next to their mother, pushing each other out of the way in their hurry. There was something very soothing about watching this fight for survival at such an early age. Ryan had had to fight to survive in the same way in the children's home, and she had no intention of letting the Montgomerys get to her. Nothing and no one was going to stop her using that beautiful studio.

She dressed with care for dinner, having brought a

couple of long skirts and contrasting tops with her, just in case she was invited up to the house while she was here. She was glad she had now that she was actually living in it!

She wore a long black woodgrain skirt, the pale blue of her silky blouse deepening the colour of her eyes, making her hair appear more golden than usual; her make-up was light, her lip-gloss the palest plum-colour.

She looked quite respectable as she gazed at herself in the full-length mirror, not at all like a Bohemian! Oh, how that rankled, the sheer arrogance and bias used in the judgment angering her. To Grant Montgomery she was an artist, and it naturally followed that she was untidy and without morals too.

Only Mandy was in the lounge when she entered the room several minutes later, and she offered no explanation for Grant's absence. But it soon became obvious where he had been; a car sounded in the driveway, and then footsteps out in the hallway. But she needn't have worried about facing him again, because accompanying Grant when he opened the double doors was a tall raven-haired woman of about his own age, an exquisitely beautiful woman, even if her brown eyes were a little hard as they flickered over Ryan. Probably pricing her skirt and blouse to the last penny, she thought bitchily. The woman's own clinging black dress looked like a couture model, the sort where you never looked at the price tag—because it didn't have one!

Grant looked very impressive in a black evening suit, the snowy white of his shirt emphasising his rugged tan, his eyes appearing greener than ever. He really was a magnificent specimen of manhood, and in his dinner suit he took Ryan's breath away. How much more lethal he would be if he were actually charming too!

The woman at his side seemed to read her thoughts; her hand was possessive on his arm, her eyes narrowing suspiciously. 'Introduce us, darling,' she said throatily.

He did so smoothly. 'Valerie Chatham, Ryan Shelton.'

'I'm so pleased to meet you.' Valerie's voice lacked sincerity, and she made no effort to offer her hand. 'You didn't bring Mark with you?' Her arched eyebrows rose censoriously.

'He's busy. In London,' Ryan replied abruptly.

'Isn't he always?' the other woman taunted. 'Shall we go in to dinner now, Grant darling? I'm sure that, like most young people, Miss Shelton is starving.'

Ryan bit her tongue to stop the caustic comment she had been going to make back, and looked up to meet Mandy's amused hazel eyes, a certain sympathy for her in their depths. Maybe against the beautiful Valerie they could be allies?

The older woman certainly went out of her way to be condescending during dinner. And she made sure that Ryan was no longer under any misapprehension as to who she was; her claim on Grant was made time and time again, both physically and verbally. Grant's expression remained bland as he smoothly played the part of perfect host, and Ryan used the word 'played' in her mind deliberately. Grant gave every impression of being lazily relaxed, and yet his gaze, whenever she happened to encounter it, was rapier-sharp. Nothing escaped his attention, not even her nervousness when she dropped her napkin, nor the way her hand on her wineglass shook slightly as his gaze lingered on her longer than usual.

She blushed as that same enigmatic gaze lingered on her once they all returned to the drawing-room, and she wondered at his thoughts behind those shuttered green eyes.

Valerie's expression hardened as she intercepted that look. 'Shouldn't we be going now, darling?' she prompted Grant. 'We did tell Giles and Anna we'd put in an appearance after their dinner party.'

He looked away from Ryan with effort. 'Of course.' He rose slowly to his feet. 'Perhaps Ryan and Mandy would like to come too?' he looked at them both enquiringly.

She liked the way he said her name; she had been startled the first time he had called her it during dinner, but somehow it sounded right in his deep gravelly voice. Somehow she found it hard to use the same informality with him, and did not call him anything.

'I doubt it.' Valerie's harsh voice interrupted her thoughts. 'The company would be a little—old for their tastes, darling.'

'Of course,' he nodded abruptly. 'If you'll excuse us, girls?'

Mandy managed to keep a straight face for as long as it took the other couple to leave the room, then she burst out laughing. 'Poor Grant,' she giggled. 'Valerie likes to give him the impression he's as old as Methuselah,' she explained, suddenly sobering. 'The only trouble is, he's beginning to fall for it!'

The air of sophistication was gone from the other girl now, and Ryan found she liked her better without it.

Mandy grimaced. 'She's trying to convince him that he should get married, before he's too old.'

'But he isn't old,' Ryan frowned.

'I keep telling him that, but he won't listen. I can't imagine anything worse than having Valerie as a sister-in-law—unless it's having you as one!' she added insultingly before leaving the room.

Ryan's gasp was for her own benefit only, as she was suddenly left alone. That last shot had been totally unexpected, and it had had all the more effect because of it. Mandy knew exactly when and where to throw her little poison arrows. So much for liking her!

With a shrug of resignation Ryan made her way to her bedroom, feeling suddenly weary. And yet so much had happened, her mind was still so active, that she was still awake when Grant returned shortly after twelve.

What a strange man he was, enigmatic and remote, a very deep man indeed. Although he made no effort to hide his opinion of artists!

She could hear him walking up the stairs now, a door opening some distance away, and then the sound of a shower being run. Did he and the beautiful Valerie sleep together? She wouldn't be surprised, Valerie's possessiveness seemed to stem from experience of an intimate relationship. And yet she hadn't persuaded him into marriage yet. Ryan wondered why she hadn't.

Suddenly a soulful noise broke the stillness of the night, a sound she had already heard once today. It was Ragtag howling again!

Oh dear, he was going to wake the whole household if she didn't stop him!

CHAPTER THREE

Ryan thrust her feet into her slippers and ran down the stairs in an effort to get down quickly and stop Ragtag making that terrible noise.

What on earth had upset him now? He had seemed all right when she had taken out his second bowl of food earlier, had been settling down for a sleep when she had left him. There was more to being a dog-owner than she had realised!

There was a bright moon tonight, and once her eyes became accustomed to the light she could see clearly. Ragtag sat in the open stable doorway, stopping his howling to give her a sorrowful look as she reached his side.

'It's no good looking at me like that,' she scolded. 'You're disturbing everyone!' Including the horses, by the sound of it, she could hear them snorting and shuffling about in their stalls. 'Now what's the matter?' she pretended anger, although really her heart had softened as soon as he licked her hand. 'Why don't you go to sleep?' she added pleadingly. 'I'm feeling tired, even if you aren't.'

He seemed calm enough now that she was down here with him. But as soon as she turned to leave he set up the howling again.

She hurried back to his side. 'Stop it, Ragtag!' she instructed crossly. 'I can't stay down here with you all night,' she murmured into his fur as she bent down to cuddle him after her show of anger. He had looked so hurt! 'Unless you would like me to sleep in the stable too?' she sighed.

'It might keep the dog quiet,' drawled the familiar voice of Grant Montgomery, 'but I don't think it's a good idea.'

Ryan spun round, almost falling over in her haste. And it was embarrassing enough already without that!

She hadn't thought she would see anyone, had thought everyone else was in bed, and her cotton nightgown was hardly adequate clothing to be wearing in front of a man she had only met this afternoon. Not that he could see through the white material, and the style was very demure, it just put her at a complete disadvantage—besides making her feel utterly ridiculous!

She stood up slowly, quietening Ragtag as he began to growl. Whenever Grant put in an appearance he began to growl, and although she might feel like doing the same herself on occasion, it was still embarrassing that he only did it to this man.

She gave Grant a nervy smile. 'I was only joking.'

His mouth twisted. 'I should hope so!'

He might have gone to his room several minutes ago, but he was still wearing the black trousers to his dinner suit, the jacket had been discarded, his tie had gone too, and several buttons on his shirt were undone. He had probably been undressing for his shower when he heard Ragtag.

'What's wrong with him?' He looked down at the now quiet dog.

'I—He doesn't seem to like sleeping on his own.'

'Do any of us?' he drawled huskily.

Ryan blushed deeply red. It was as if Grant had picked up the intimacy of the situation from her; his whole manner was different from the way he had behaved earlier today, reminding her of those probing glances he had been giving her all through dinner. She had later dismissed those looks as just her imagination, now she wasn't so sure.

But surely Valerie Chatham could more than satisfy him physically. He had taken the other woman out over two hours ago, but that didn't mean they had been at the party all that time. His remark about not sleeping alone seemed to confirm her belief that he and Valerie were lovers. Then why was he looking at her like this?

'Ryan?' he prompted softly at her lengthy silence.

'I—I don't know what to do with him,' she stumbled over her words, feelings decidedly uncomfortable now. The nightgown might be a modest one, but she, at least, was aware that she was naked beneath it. She had a feeling Grant knew she was too.

'He won't sleep down here?'

She grimaced. 'It doesn't look like it.'

'Then take him to your room,' he shrugged.

Her eyes widened. 'Rex and Riba,' she reminded him. Having met the two dogs earlier, a beautiful pair of Golden Labradors, she could quite understand their disgust with the disreputable Ragtag.

'They won't even know he's in the house if you keep him in your room,' Grant answered.

'But he's dirty——'

'Do you want to take him into the house or don't you?' he snapped his impatience.

'I do—of course I do,' she blushed.

'Then do so.' He turned on his heel and walked off.

Ryan watched him go in dismay. He had been attempting to be friendly, and she had bungled it. 'Come on, Ragtag,' she said dejectedly, 'let's get to bed.'

He seemed quite happy now he was to come into the house, making her wonder at the ease with which he had got his own way. He might be scruffy to look at, but it didn't prevent him achieving his objective. Although she had to admit to being slightly surprised at the way Grant Montgomery had given in. After his earlier attitude she had thought he wished both Ragtag and herself far away from here.

She was even more surprised when she went into the kitchen to find him in there.

'Coffee,' he explained as he turned from the percolator, and his eyes narrowed as he looked at her in the full light. 'I think you could do with some too,' he derided her chattering teeth. 'It might be April, Ryan, but it's hardly warm enough at night to walk about like that.'

She had realised that as soon as she entered the warm kitchen; the cold seemed to have entered her bones. 'I was in a hurry to stop Ragtag,' she blushed.

'Well, now you can relax. Sit down.'

'Oh no! I—I'm not dressed.'

Mockery deepened the deep green of his eyes. 'I don't mind if you don't,' he drawled, putting the two cups of coffee on the kitchen table.

It smelt delicious, and she did need warming up. But she couldn't sit down with him like this. What if someone should come in? Mandy, for example. What construction would she put on the situation? 'I'll go and put my housecoat on,' she decided firmly.

'Please yourself,' Grant shrugged, sitting down to drink his own coffee. 'Or take it with you if you want to.'

She didn't particularly want to. Her tiredness of earlier had passed, and besides, it seemed churlish of her after he had allowed Ragtag in the house. 'I'll only be a moment,' she said softly.

He seemed not to hear her, his hands cupping the

mug as he slowly sipped the hot drink, his thoughts inwards. Ryan had an impression of loneliness in that moment, which was ridiculous in the circumstances. Grant had numerous servants, a brother and sister who loved him, and Valerie, who certainly wanted to marry him. He didn't need her sympathy!

Ragtag lost no time in jumping on to the bottom of her bed once they reached her room, resisting all her efforts to push him off. 'That bedspread is *pink*, you silly dog!' she groaned, knowing that it wouldn't be pink much longer. 'Get off,' she ordered firmly, having to witness the indignity of the dog falling asleep even as she spoke to him. 'Having Grant Montgomery see me like this was all your fault, and you have the nerve to go to sleep!' She might as well have saved her breath, for the dog didn't even twitch an ear. 'I'll remember this next feeding time!' she warned him as she left, adequately covered by her housecoat now.

Grant had moved to pour himself another cup of coffee, the mockery still in his eyes as he took in the navy blue robe. 'Feel better?' he taunted.

'Yes, thank you.' She avoided his gaze, stirring sugar into her cooling coffee.

'Where's the dog?' He sat down opposite her.

'Asleep upstairs,' she grimaced.

'He likes his creature comforts.' His mouth quirked.

'Yes.'

'So, how long have you known Mark?' The question was casually put, and yet the green eyes had norrowed intently.

'About eighteen months,' she replied as casually.

'Strange, he's never mentioned you before.'

Ryan withstood his steely look with a calm that was only a veneer. Grant's politeness was only as skin-deep as Mandy's had been, he liked her no better than his sister did. 'Maybe I wasn't important enough,' she shrugged.

'Perhaps,' he nodded. 'Although that doesn't appear to be the case now.'

She put her cup down, sighing. 'Look, maybe I should tell you, Mark is——'

'You don't owe me any explanations, Ryan,' he interrupted. 'If there are any to be made Mark will make them.' His tone was inflexible, there was a hard anger in his face.

That he was annoyed with his young brother she could tell, and she could probably even give part of the reason why! Herself. 'I think I'll go to bed now. Thank you for the—Oh!' she gasped as his hand came out to grasp her about the wrist. 'Grant?' she frowned down at him.

'Sit down. Please,' he added at her indignant gasp, releasing her as she slowly sat down again. 'I just feel I should warn you that there's also a girl called Diana in Mark's life, a girl he sounds serious about.'

'Yes?' Ryan was wary now.

'Yes. I wouldn't want you to get hurt.'

'No?' Her tone was dry now.

His eyes narrowed, but her expression became deliberately bland. Wouldn't want her to get hurt, indeed! What on earth was the matter with this family, didn't they want Mark to be happy? First one of them warned her off Mark, then the other one did. Why did they keep trying to protect a fully grown man who was perfectly capable of taking care of himself?

'Mark is—has been unreliable, in the past,' Grant told her woodenly.

'Really?'

'Yes,' he said tersely, sensing her scepticism. 'I

don't think you're taking me seriously, Ryan,' he scowled at her across the table.

'Oh yes, I am.' She stood up, this time receiving no objection from him. 'Mark is unreliable. And anyway, you think he has another woman. Isn't that right so far?' She eyed him mockingly.

'You think I'm being over-cautious——'

'I'm *sure* you are.' There was a brittle hardness to her voice.

'Mark has a reputation for falling in and out of love——'

'And you don't want me to be hurt!' she scorned.

Grant's breath entered his body with an angry hiss, the broad shoulders stiffened, his eyes were glacial. 'Do you think you would be the first of his girl-friends to come crying on my shoulder when it's over?' he rasped. 'First it was Suzy, then Gina, then Jane, then——'

'All right, you've made your point,' she said through gritted teeth. 'Although why any of those girls should want to cry on *your* shoulder I have no idea! Why don't you just have a little faith in your brother, maybe this time it will be different?' It had better be, because if he hurt Diana she would personally throttle him!

'Maybe,' he agreed grimly. 'Although I very much doubt it. Are you and Mark lovers, is that it?'

'Certainly not!' Ryan gasped. 'How dare you?'

He ran a weary hand over his eyes. 'I'm not sure. Perhaps it would be better if you forgot we had this little—chat.'

'Don't tell Mark, you mean?' Her eyes flashed in a warning of her rising temper.

'I think that would be best,' he nodded.

'For whom? You, I think! Does Mark know you do

this little warning off job? I doubt it,' she scorned. 'You see, Mark is basically a very honest person, he doesn't believe in intrigue and lies.'

'He will also be a very rich young man very soon, sooner if he marries,' Grant ground out, as angry as she now.

'How lucky for him, then,' she almost shouted. 'Because he intends marrying *very soon*!'

Now she knew the reason for the warning! Both Grant and Mandy believed her to be after Mark's money. They weren't concerned about her at all, they just didn't want a gold-digger in the family! Poor Diana would have a fit if she were faced with the same opposition, her vulnerability where families were concerned was very fragile. Mark had known that, and suddenly his invitation for her to stay here no longer seemed quite so innocent. She would call him first thing tomorrow and find out what game he was playing—with her as the pawn!

'Does he now?' Grant towered to his feet. 'He hasn't mentioned it to me.'

'Really?' she snapped. 'But then you aren't exactly in Mark's confidence, are you?' she taunted, more angry than she had been for a long time.

His eyes glittered. 'And you are?'

'Oh yes,' she told him with confidence, knowing that she was as close to Mark as any of the other students, more so because of his friendship with Diana. 'Mark and I are very close,' she added provocatively.

'You think you're very clever, don't you, Ryan?' Grant rasped furiously. 'You think Mark will marry you, but I can assure you he won't.'

So could she—if this man weren't so darned arrogant. 'We'll just have to wait and see, won't we?' she challenged.

'Yes,' he bit out furiously, even the veneer of politeness gone now. 'Perhaps this will help your waiting!' He pulled her roughly against him to kiss her brutally on the mouth.

Ryan knew the drugging movement of his mouth on hers was supposed to be an insult, and yet her response was involuntary. She seemed to have no control over her body, curving her slender frame against him, her arms moving up about his neck.

The tip of his tongue probed the edge of her mouth, their response to each other was all the more intense because of their deep anger. But anger was soon replaced with passion, a passion that seemed explosive as Grant's mouth fused with hers once again, his hands moving in fevered exploration over her slender curves, pushing aside her robe to place a hand possessively over her taut breast.

'Grant!' She pulled back with a gasp.

For a moment his eyes gleamed down at her like black coals, and then he was kissing her again, devouring her with his lips, uncaring of the fact that he despised her, that they had only met that afternoon.

Ryan had never known such sensation. Her skin seemed to burn where he touched her, her senses reeling from the sensuality of his probing mouth.

Their hearts beat a loud tattoo of uncontrolled passion, and Ryan gasped as she felt Grant probing the neckline of her nightgown, feeling the beat of her heart for himself, his fingers erotic against her hardened nipple.

No man had ever touched her this intimately, not even Alan, whom she had loved so much, and it was finally shock at her wanton behaviour that made her pull back.

To her shame Grant was looking down at her with

cool green eyes, the arousal of his body in complete contrast to the disgust she could read in his expression. 'Enough?' he drawled insultingly.

Ryan swallowed hard, her lips swollen with passion, realising how easily she had succumbed to his lovemaking. 'You're despicable!' she choked.

He didn't dispute the fact. 'I'm also Mark's brother. How do you think he would feel about what happened just now?'

She met the challenge in his eyes with effort. 'I'll ask him the next time I speak to him,' she returned coolly.

His mouth twisted. 'I doubt it.'

'No?' Her brows rose.

'No,' he scorned mockingly, very sure of himself.

She gave a haughty inclination of her head. 'I'll let you know what he says as soon as I've spoken to him.' She turned to leave the room.

'Ryan!' He waited as she slowly turned, a tall dominating man who seconds ago had aroused her deliberately, who had intended to humiliate her. 'Don't try and cause trouble between Mark and me,' he advised grimly. 'You simply aren't important enough. You're just the last in a long line of promiscuous young women who briefly held my brother enthralled,' he dismissed contemptuously. 'He'll never marry you,' he repeated his earlier claim.

She didn't answer him—she couldn't; her emotions were a confusing mixture of anger and pain. She knew she was a little nobody and so not important to the Grant Montgomerys of the world, but she certainly wasn't promiscuous. It was the last that angered her. Grant thought that because she had responded to him she slept around. But he had responded to her too, so what did that make him!

Ryan had slept badly, dark circles beneath the blue of her eyes, her cheeks pale. She could remember every moment of being in Grant Montgomery's arms, and her relief was immense when she got downstairs the next morning to find she had the dining-room to herself; the maid informed her that Grant was working on the estate, and Mandy was out riding.

She took Ragtag outside and fed him before coming back for her coffee, but ignored the salvers of food, not feeling hungry. Grant had succeeded in humiliating her last night, and somehow she was going to have to act as if nothing had happened between them. Mainly for her own satisfaction, but also because Mandy was an astute young lady, and she wouldn't fail to notice any strain in the atmosphere between Grant and herself. Mandy's taunts on top of her brother's she could do without.

She called Mark straight after finishing her coffee, using the telephone in the drawing-room so that she shouldn't be overheard. Luckily he answered almost straight away.

'Ryan!' he recognised her voice. 'Anything wrong?'

'You know there is,' she said tightly. 'You conniving, irresponsible, thoughtless——'

'Hey, what have I done?' Puzzlement sharpened his voice.

'You know full well——'

'If I did I wouldn't be asking,' he sighed. 'Although—My big brother hasn't been picking on you already, has he?' he asked in an incredulous voice.

'Right first time,' she said grimly.

'Well, he didn't waste much time!'

'Well?'

'Oh, Ryan, look I didn't mean to use you as a scapegoat——'

'But?' she prompted hardly.

'They'd break Diana,' he said desperately. 'Surely you can see that? I only mentioned her to Grant once last month and he was instantly suspicious of her. Until I'm more sure of her myself I'm not willing to expose her to Grant and Mandy. My little sister hero-worships Grant, thinks he can do no wrong, and so she follows his example of putting my girl-friends down. Most of them turn tail and run in the face of their hostility.'

'And me?'

'Ah, now you're a different matter,' the smile could be heard in his voice. 'I've never known you to run away from anything, least of all a fight. I knew what Grant and Mandy would think when you arrived, in fact I hoped they would think that.'

'Dare I ask why?' Ryan put in dryly, feeling as if she were on a roller-coaster that had run away with her.

'Diversion,' he replied instantly. 'Diana is stubborn, and once she's made her mind up no one will change it. But until she does she's very vulnerable. If she even guessed there might be opposition to us getting married she'd probably stop seeing me right now.'

How well he knew Diana! She hadn't realised that under Mark's lighthearted flirting he had somehow managed to probe the very depth of Diana's nature. The knowledge reassured her of his sincerity.

'There's only one problem,' she frowned. 'When your brother—' she couldn't bring herself to call him Grant!—'when he was warning me off you last night,' was it only last night that he had kissed her so passionately?—'he told me you were serious about someone called Diana.'

'Probably the first name he thought of,' Mark dismissed.

'He also mentioned the names Suzy, Gina, and Jane,' she mocked.

'He did?'

'Yes, he did,' she smiled at the grimace that could be heard in his voice, her anger leaving her.

'Trust Grant,' he muttered. 'All right, so I did go out with them in the past, but you know that for the past six months I haven't looked at anyone else but Diana. I'm twenty-four, Ryan, of course there've been other girls in my life. And, Grant hasn't exactly led a blameless life himself!'

'I met his girl-friend last night.'

'Valerie,' Mark said disgustedly. 'He likes to interfere in my life where he had no right to, but even so I wouldn't wish Valerie on him! He can't seem to see the viper in her.'

'Oh, I wouldn't go that far——'

'I would,' he derided. 'Valerie has it in her mind that she should be the next mistress of Montgomery Hall, and so far Grant hasn't put up any objections. For once Mandy and I are in agreement, we both think she's awful.'

'Your brother obviously doesn't.'

'No. Which isn't like Grant at all. He can usually see right through people.'

'He definitely thinks he's seen through me,' Ryan grimaced. 'He thinks I'm after your money. Mark, he says you're going to inherit a lot of money soon,' she added worriedly.

'In ten months' time, when I'm twenty-five,' he confirmed cheerfully. 'Or if I marry.'

'Does Diana know?'

'No, if she did she'd certainly finish with me, would

think I wanted to marry her just to get my money. And I can assure you I don't need the money. If I had I could have married years ago to get it.'

'Mark——'

'I'll tell her before we get married, Ryan,' he assured her hastily. 'I just daren't take the risk right now. You're going to help me, aren't you?' he added pleadingly.

'As a diversion,' she sighed.

'Well, if they believe you're my girl-friend they won't think of interfering here.'

'And why aren't you here with me?' she derided.

'I have a project on at the college,' he said tongue-in-cheek. 'At least, that's what I told Grant. Do this for me, please, Ryan, and I'll let you be chief bridesmaid.'

'You don't have any say in it,' she told him with pretended indignation. 'Diana and I already arranged all that when we were still in ankle-socks!'

'I just turn up on the day, hmm?'

'If she accepts you.'

'So you'll help me—us—out?' he said hopefully.

She could see that he did need help, knew that if Diana had been subjected to Grant Montgomery's physical onslaught of last night she would have left here long ago. It wasn't that Diana was weak, as Mark said, she was very stubborn, but at the moment she didn't have enough confidence in Mark's love to withstand the pressure Grant Montgomery could bring to bear.

'All right,' she decided. 'But only for these three weeks, then you'll have to make your own plans.'

'I'm hoping to have at least persuaded Diana to get engaged by then,' he said with quiet satisfaction. 'And once I've got her to commit herself that far I know she won't back out.'

'No,' Ryan acknowledged softly.

'You'll be all right, won't you?' he asked anxiously. 'I'll be there myself next weekend, so I'll give you some moral support then.'

'Thanks! What do I do in the meantime?'

He gave a husky laugh. 'Stay out of Grant's way.'

'I intend to! Just get Diana to agree to marry you soon, I can't stand the strain.'

Mark rang off with a laugh, but Ryan sat in the drawing-room for several minutes longer. Staying out of Grant's way could be easier said than done, especially as he was so against her. But now that she had agreed to help Mark she wouldn't let him down.

She went to the studio for a while after her telephone call to Mark, and set up her canvases, just revelling in the wonder of being there, hesitant about starting work, knowing that once she did she would lose all track of time.

No one had mentioned showing her Paul Gilbert's paintings, but in the circumstances perhaps that was understandable. She would probably have to wait for Mark's arrival now.

She picked up her sketch-pad and went downstairs, collecting Ragtag from the backyard to go for a walk. He didn't appreciate being woken from his morning siesta, walking dejectedly behind her as she strolled off across the fields.

'You'll get fat if you don't have any exercise,' she warned him. He didn't look very impressed, his head was still down. 'Now don't you go falling out with me too,' she pleaded teasingly. 'You're my only friend here.'

He appeared in a better mood as she sat down beneath a tree to gaze over the open countryside. She had always believed Yorkshire to be bleak, and yet it was beautiful here, the gorse in full bloom, brightly yellow, the trees budding with the light green leaves of early spring. The sun shone down warmly now that she was out of the wind, and she opened her sketch-pad to capture the beauty of the scene before her. There was something exhilarating about being here, lightening her heart.

Ragtag slept beside her as the morning passed in quiet enjoyment, occasionally opening an eye if any of the sleepy bees that were buzzing about flew too close to him; the bleating of the lambs did not seem to bother him at all.

It wasn't until almost lunch-time that Ryan realised she hadn't given Alan a thought all day. A month ago he had been very important in her life, yet today she hadn't even thought of him! Maybe it was the peace here, or the situation she found herself in because of Mark—or maybe it was just the memory of demanding lips on her own that put Alan from her mind. She couldn't seem to stop thinking about Grant Montgomery!

He had been brutal, deliberately so, and yet she couldn't get him out of her mind!

'Let's go, Ragtag.' She stood up forcefully, her concentration disturbed. 'Lunch-time,' she told him encouragingly. 'And this afternoon,' she added softly, 'I'm going to give you a bath. You're not only dirty, dog, you're also a little on the smelly side!'

Ragtag didn't seem alarmed by the word 'bath', so she doubted if he had ever had one before. He didn't know what a treat he had in store later today!

Mandy was coming out of the stable as Ryan walked into the yard, and after the way they had parted last night she wasn't too sure how to greet the other girl.

Mandy felt no such inhibition; her face was glowing from her ride. 'Had a good morning?' she smiled, looking younger and more relaxed today.

'Er—Yes, thank you.' To say she was surprised—and wary—of the other girl's friendliness would be an understatement.

Mandy had worn denims and a checked shirt to go riding, and her cheeks were flushed and her short hair windswept. 'I was rude to you last night,' she said softly. 'I'm sorry.'

'I—Well—That's all right,' Ryan stumbled over her words.

'I didn't mean it either,' the other girl grimaced. 'There's just no comparison between you and Valerie.'

'Thanks—I think,' Ryan frowned.

'Yes, it was a compliment,' Mandy laughed. 'Now you're wondering why, aren't you?' she smiled. 'Oh, don't worry, I'm not suddenly turning over a new leaf, I'll probably be my usual bitchy self later, I just think the remark I made last night was uncalled for. Besides being a little premature?' She quirked one dark brow.

Ryan's expression lightened. 'It could be,' she answered noncommittally, remembering her role.

The other girl shrugged. 'I can't blame you for not wanting to confide in me, I wouldn't want to in the circumstances either. But Grant's pretty steamed up about it, I can tell.'

Ryan already knew that, only last night she had witnessed one of the boiling rages Mandy had warned her about. 'I already guessed that,' she derided.

'I suppose you did,' Mandy nodded. 'Oh well, I'll see you at lunch. I have to go and get cleaned up.'

So did Ryan, and she once again left Ragtag outside, finding that he seemed all right outside in the day, as long as he realised she was in the house and so not far away. Ryan had never had someone so totally dependent on her for emotional comfort before, and she liked the feeling. She only hoped Diana wasn't going to mind a dog about the place when she got back to London, although she was pretty certain she wouldn't. They both had a liking for animals, and at the children's home they had never had any, except the communally owned tomcat, who had seemed to spend more time increasing his own species than charming the children.

She was quite pleased with the sketches she had done this morning, although she was nowhere near starting the painting she had in mind; she wanted to get exactly the right setting before she did that.

Still, she was hungry now. The Sunday roast had smelt delicious as she walked through the reception area of the house to the stairs, Mandy having already disappeared into her room.

She was nowhere to be seen now, and Ryan had no idea whether Grant would be joining them for lunch. As she opened the drawing-room door she had her answer. Not only was Grant joining them, but Valerie Chatham was too. The two of them were kissing quite passionately as Ryan looked at them in dismay!

CHAPTER FOUR

Even as she turned to walk away Grant was raising his head, his eyes narrowing as he saw her in the open doorway. Valerie turned to follow his line of vision, her eyes flashing her dislike as she too saw Ryan.

'Really, Grant,' she moved gracefully away from him, smoothing her hair, 'It's impossible to get any privacy in this house lately!'

'I'm sure Ryan didn't mean to interrupt,' he drawled, looking totally unmoved by the fact that he had just been seen kissing the other woman very passionately indeed, their bodies curved together, their arms about each other.

It was the first time Ryan had seen him since he had kissed *her*, since he had treated her so contemptuously, talking to her so cruelly. But she refused to so much as blush, and walked completely into the drawing-room to close the door behind her. 'Maybe you should put a notice up on the door,' she said lightly.

Anger flashed in Grant's eyes. 'I didn't feel it necessary in my own home,' he snapped.

Ryan sat down, looking up at them coolly, glad that she had put on a nice summery skirt and deep blue tee-shirt, although she was aware that it in no way compared with the cut and style of Valerie Chatham's tailored skirt and silk blouse.

Having expected her to make some cutting retort to his angry outburst, she could see she had disconcerted him by her silence, meeting his narrow-eyed gaze with a calmness she was far from feeling. But if she were to act this part for Mark she was going to have to start off by standing up to his autocratic brother. Letting him see he could daunt her at the first opportunity wasn't going to help Mark at all.

Valerie Chatham seemed to have totally mis-interpreted her silence, and gave her a rather catty smile of triumph.

'So what did you do with your morning?' Grant asked Ryan hardly.

She shrugged. 'I went up to the studio, then for a walk. And, of course, I spoke to Mark.'

He seemed to stiffen. 'Really?' he said guardedly.

'Mm,' she nodded. 'He sent his love,' she added mockingly, watching the dark hue colour his lean cheeks.

'Indeed?' he rasped.

'Yes.' She was enjoying this, for once feeling as if she had the upper hand with Grant Montgomery. He was desperate to know whether or not she had told Mark he had kissed her, as she had threatened she would. 'I assured him how welcome you'd all made me feel.'

His jaw tightened. 'I'm glad you feel that way.'

'Oh yes,' a light of revenge entered her eyes, 'especially your kindness late last night when you insisted on making me a cup of coffee. It was very nice of you.'

'Grant . . .?' Valerie gasped.

'Especially as I was hardly dressed for it,' Ryan continued with feigned innocence. 'I felt a little conspicuous sitting with you in my nightgown. Still, we're both adults,' she looked at him challengingly, knowing by the angry glitter in his eyes, the rigidness of his jaw, that she had almost pushed him to the limit for one day. It was enough that she had shown him she wouldn't be pushed around. 'And I'm sure you've seen plenty of women in less,' she added with a bright smile.

'Grant!' Valerie was openly angry now, her mouth tight.

'Yes?' He looked at the other woman coldly, daring her to question his movements.

Her gaze fell from his, and she shot Ryan a look of intense dislike. 'Shall we go in to lunch?' she suggested tautly.

At that Mandy walked into the room, changed from her riding clothes now, wearing a tailored silky dress in a particularly attractive shade of green. 'Are you waiting for me?' she said brightly, sensing none of the undercurrents of antagonism that existed between the other three as they ate their meal, conversation virtually non-existent.

But Ryan knew of Grant's anger, knew there would be retribution for the way she had attempted to embarrass him in front of Valerie Chatham. And he hadn't been embarrassed. He had been furious with her, but he felt he owed the other woman no explanation. Ryan felt sure he would demand one from *her* before the day was through.

When the other couple left shortly after lunch Ryan for one heaved a sigh of relief, and Mandy didn't look too bothered by their departure either.

'I wonder what they've argued about,' she said uninterestedly.

The two of them were sitting in the drawing-room. Ryan looked at the other girl curiously. 'Do they argue a lot?'

Mandy shrugged. 'Quite a bit. Do you and Mark argue?'

'Never,' she answered without hesitation.

'Do you love him?'

'I—In a way,' she amended her flat denial. After all, if Mark did marry Diana he would be an honorary brother-in-law, for she and Diana were like sisters.

Mandy grimaced and stood up. 'Everyone seems to have someone to love but me. Sleaton isn't exactly teeming with sexy-looking men,' she derided.

'There's Peter Thornby.'

Mandy looked at her sharply, forcing the tension to leave her as she met Ryan's deliberately bland expression. 'He's always too busy to notice anything but his patients. What are you going to do this afternoon?' she changed the subject.

Ryan respected her wish not to talk about the young vet. 'I thought I might bathe Ragtag.'

'Not before time!'

'No,' she laughed lightly. 'That's what I thought.'

'I should change out of those clothes if I were you,' Mandy advised. 'I've helped Grant with Rex and Riba in the past, and you tend to get in rather a mess yourself.'

She took the other girl's advice, and put on her oldest denims and tee-shirt, both splattered with paint, not being really too worried if they were messed up. She secured her hair at her nape too.

She found Ragtag outside having his afternoon nap—in fact, he seemed to spend the whole of his life sleeping!

'I have a lovely surprise for you,' she told him as he looked up at her, and went into the stable to take down the metal bath from the wall that Mandy had told her Grant used for the Labradors.

The dog watched her movements with interest as she began to carry the water over in a bucket from the tap inside the stable, having placed the tin bath outside in the yard. Ragtag had an aversion to going into the stable at the best of times, and Ryan knew she would never be able to carry the bath outside once it had the water in. Nevertheless, after the fifth bucketful she was beginning to think Ragtag would have to take his bath where she put it. It was hell on her back carrying this bucket!

'What on earth are you doing?'

Ryan looked up in the middle of carrying her eighth bucketful to the bath, glaring her dislike at Grant as he watched her struggles. 'What does it look like?' she said fiercely, emptying the water and straightening with an effort, every muscle in her back seeming to ache.

'Why didn't you use the hose?' he drawled.

She blinked. 'What hose?'

He strode into the stable, coming back seconds later with a coiled green hosepipe. 'This one,' he mocked.

Ryan could have cried. It had taken her almost an hour to fill the bath, with the use of the hose it would have taken a matter of minutes! 'No one told me about it,' she snapped badtemperedly.

He shrugged his broad shoulders. 'It was hanging on the wall just inside.'

'Well, I didn't see it!'

'Obviously.'

She glared up at him, hating him for his superiority. 'Has Miss Chatham gone home?'

His jaw tightened, the amusement leaving his eyes. 'Yes, she's gone home. That was rather a cheap shot you made earlier,' he rasped.

'About as cheap as the one you made last night,' Ryan nodded.

Grant's mouth twisted. 'I don't remember you thinking it cheap at the time. In fact, I seem to remember you liked it.'

'I seem to remember a similar reaction in you.' She scorned to hide her embarrassment, unable to deny the truth.

Grant didn't deny it either. His stance was challenging, the black denims and black silk shirt giving him the look of the devil himself. 'Maybe we should explore that—liking, at a more convenient time?' he drawled softly, his green eyes caressing on the soft curve of her face.

'Have you forgotten Miss Chatham?' she mocked.

'Have you forgotten Mark?'

'Not at all,' she flashed. 'He's always in my thoughts. Now, if you'll excuse me, I intend bathing Ragtag.'

'That might be rather difficult,' Grant taunted.

She looked at him sharply. 'Why?'

'I think he's realised what you're doing, he just disappeared around the side of the stable!'

Ryan turned with a gasp. Ragtag had indeed gone! 'Damn, damn, *damn*!' If she hadn't had an audience in the shape of Grant Montgomery she would probably have stamped her foot too! She glared at him. 'I've just broken my back carrying that water out here, and *you* come along and frighten my dog off!'

His eyes widened at the injustice of her accusation, then he began to smile, the smile turning into a full-throated laugh, throwing his head back with obvious enjoyment.

Ryan dropped the bucket on the cobbles, breathing hard in her anger, too furious to notice how handsome he looked, his genuine humour making him appear younger, a cleft in one of his lean cheeks as he continued to smile, his teeth very white against his dark skin, his eyes a luminous green.

Ryan noticed none of that; her own face was flushed with fury. 'What are you laughing at?'

He sobered with an effort. 'You look like a little girl when you're angry.'

'Really?' she said in a dangerously soft voice.

'Really.' He began to smile again.

This time Ryan did notice how devastating he looked, and her breath seemed to be knocked from her body. This man was lethal when he forgot to be cruel. She couldn't possibly be becoming attracted to him! That wouldn't help Mark at all. No, she mustn't allow herself to be attracted to such a man. He could destroy her if he chose to.

She turned away. 'I'd better try and find Ragtag,' she mumbled, 'or the water will be cold.'

'Of course.' He was once again the rigidly formal man she was used to. 'I have some shampoo you can use, I'll get it for you. I use it on the Labradors.'

'Where are they?' she frowned. Considering they were supposed to live here they were rarely about!

'With my estate manager.' He gave a half smile. 'I don't think they're quite sure which one of us they belong to. When I'm away he takes care of them.'

'And do you go away often?'

'Often enough,' he revealed haughtily. 'I'll get the shampoo for you.' He turned and walked away.

Ryan began searching for Ragtag, determinedly not thinking about the way Grant had briefly dropped his contemptuous attitude towards her. It could be too disturbing!

A few minutes later she heard a horse leaving the stable, and turned just in time to see Grant astride a black stallion, looking more like the devil as he rode away, bent low over the stallion's back.

'Was that Grant I heard just now?' Mandy came across the yard towards her, once again in her riding clothes.

'Mm,' she answered absently, reading the instructions on the back of the bottle Grant had left out for her, hoping that Ragtag would return of his own accord. She certainly wasn't having any luck finding him! When he wanted to disappear he did it without trace.

'*Laughing*?' Mandy sounded incredulous.

Ryan gave a surprised laugh herself. 'Don't look so shocked.'

'I'm not. It's just——' Mandy frowned. 'He doesn't laugh like that very often. Usually it's just a twist of his mouth when he's amused, or a cynical smile. It's years since I heard him laugh like that,' she revealed.

'He seems to find me funny,' Ryan said dryly. 'Or at least, the fact that I have a temper.'

'I don't care *what* made him laugh, I'm just glad it happened. It was good to hear.'

Ryan shrugged. 'Who knows, maybe he'll find other things about me that amuse him.'

'Ryan——'

'There you are, you silly dog!' Ryan pounced on Ragtag as he appeared back round the stable, holding on to him. 'Help me get him in the bath, will you?' she pleaded with Mandy.

'I—Oh, all right,' she gave in. 'But I warn you, we'll both get soaked.'

It was a warning that was to come overwhelmingly true. Ragtag fought all their efforts to bath him calmly, merely suffering the scrubbing of his fur, then he got out of the bath to shake his long coat all over Mandy.

She backed off with a squeal, but it was already too late, she was wetter than ever, her clothes clinging to her wetly, water literally dripping from her hair.

'Great!' she grimaced, starting to shiver despite the

sun. 'I think I'm wetter than he is!'

Ryan began to laugh, and soon Mandy was joining in, the two of them having dropped all hostilities while they bathed the dog, needing all their strength to keep him in one place.

Ryan began to rub Ragtag's long fur dry, Mandy having found an old blanket in the stable she could use. 'He looks better now, though, doesn't he?' she looked at him admiringly, having revealed a snowy white and smoky grey coat.

'He looks beautiful,' Mandy agreed, still smiling. 'Now we'd better chase him round the yard a bit before you brush him. It will dry him off,' she explained.

The silly dog thought it great fun to be chased round and round the yard, finally collapsing outside the kitchen door, looking up expectantly.

'I think he wants feeding,' Mandy said breathlessly.

'Not until I've brushed him.' Ryan collapsed next to him, the brush in her hand. 'I think you should go and get changed, before you catch pneumonia.' The other girl was still very wet, despite their mad antics.

'You're a little wet yourself,' Mandy derided.

Mandy certainly was; her tee-shirt was now clinging to her, clearly outlining the curve of her breast in fine detail. 'I'll change when I've cleared away out here. You're worse than me, anyway. Go on and have a shower, I shouldn't be long.' She began to brush Ragtag.

By the time she had finished he did truly look beautiful, a really regal-looking Old English Sheepdog. But he didn't look quite so regal when he threw himself at his food-bowl!

Ryan left him to it and went over to empty the bath, carrying it back into the stable, reaching up to put it on the wall.

'Let me,' Grant murmured behind her, taking it from her shaking hands to put it on the hook.

Ryan stood uncomfortably within the circle of his arms; she could feel the warmth of his body against hers, the smell of horseflesh and human perspiration, a heady mixture in any circumstances, dangerously so with Grant.

She turned awkwardly in his arms, bringing their thighs together, and flinched back from him, but she only came up against the wall, looking up at him beneath lowered lashes. His hair was windswept, a healthy colour to his harsh cheeks, his breathing becoming shallow as he looked down at her.

'Dear girl,' he suddenly rasped, one hand moving to tentatively touch her breast, 'what on earth have you been doing? You're soaking wet!'

Ryan wetted her lips nervously with the tip of her tongue. 'I—Ragtag was a little—generous with his bath-water.' She could feel the heat of his hand through the thin cotton material of her top, and her breath caught in her throat as he hesitantly touched the hardened nipple.

He looked up as he heard her involuntary gasp of pleasure, his eyes like emeralds in the gloom at the back of this empty stall. 'I thought about you while I was out,' he told her huskily, releasing her hair so that it lay silkily on her shoulders.

Ryan was having difficulty breathing, his fingertips now teasing her body. 'You did?' she choked, pleasure threatening to spiral out of control.

'Yes,' he ground out. 'But I never thought I'd be doing this,' his hands moved beneath her tee-shirt as he stepped closer to her. 'I didn't imagine you'd be waiting for me here.'

'Oh, but I——'

His mouth on hers stopped any more talk between them, and soon, very soon, she had nothing to say, her senses singing as dizzy pleasure shot through her body, a wild sensation of longing for even closer contact between them.

Grant's mouth still moved over hers as he lowered her down into the sweet-smelling hay, his lips moving against hers, each telling of their full arousal.

Ryan's mouth moved in fevered caresses over his jaw and throat, feeling the probe of his lips against her earlobe, going lower, lower ... The air felt cool against her naked breasts as Grant smoothed the wet material back, the slight dampness of her skin heightening the sensations as his mouth claimed one taut nipple, caressing the nub, desire coursing through her body at each silken caress of his tongue.

'You're perfection!' he gasped against her flesh. 'Silky, smooth, oh, I could devour every inch of you!' He claimed her mouth again, his lips moving druggingly against hers, his hands continuing their exploration of her body, releasing the fastening on her denims to caress the softness beneath, the lacy briefs posing no problems to his questing hand.

She gasped as he touched her inner thigh, the surge of passion that engulfed her taking her breath away. She kissed his bared chest, having dispensed with the buttons on his shirt long ago, her nails digging into his back as she caressed him beneath the silk material.

A sensation such as she had never known before, a delicious pleasurable ache was taking over her body; her limbs felt weightless, only the touch of Grant's hands and mouth were important to her, nothing and no one else mattered any more.

'Touch me, Ryan,' he encouraged with a groan, moving her hand to the belt of his denims, aiding her

with the fastening as she fumbled with the task. 'Dear
God, *yes*!' he arched against her hand as she touched
him.

'Ryan? Grant?' Mandy called out uncertainly. 'Are
you in here?'

Grant's hand over her mouth prevented Ryan's
gasp of dismay being heard. 'Quiet!' he ordered
through gritted teeth. 'She'll go away in a moment,' he
hissed.

'Ryan? Grant?' Mandy repeated impatiently.

All the time they were waiting for Mandy to leave
Ryan stared up at Grant with shocked eyes, his hand
still over her mouth, her eyes her only means of
expression.

To say she was shocked was an understatement—
she was mortified! Here they both lay, both partially
unclothed, their bare flesh still entwined, although
desire had ebbed for both of them, leaving only stark
reality in its wake. She had almost shared the ultimate
physical experience with Grant Montgomery, had
almost given herself to him in a bed of straw!

Finally Mandy's footsteps could be heard leaving,
and Grant rolled away from Ryan, removing his hand
from her mouth at the same time. She was afraid to
move as he stared sightlessly up at the ceiling for
several long minutes.

'No post-mortems, no recriminations,' he rasped
finally. 'I think you should just go!'

So did she, and she scrambled inelegantly to her
feet, straightening her clothing as she did so. She ran
to the door, turning briefly, her last sight of Grant as
he still lay in the straw, the disarray of his clothes
caused by her own impatient fingers.

Luckily she saw no one else as she ran to her room,
where she leaned back weakly against the door, her

pulse-rate refusing to slow. What had just happened
had totally bewildered her, left her with a lack of faith
in herself. She would never have believed she could
behave so wantonly, never have guessed that Grant
Montgomery would be the man to have such an
explosive effect on her. She still ached for the
fulfilment she had trembled on, still wanted the
hardness of his body entwined with hers. If Mandy
hadn't come along and interrupted them . . .!

A lukewarm shower did nothing to dampen her
senses, and it was with hot cheeks and trembling body
that she left the house to walk with Ragtag.

How could she have let that happen? How could she
have stopped it! That awareness had been between
them since the previous night, and there had been no
way either of them could have denied that heated
response to each other.

Grant might have been using her last night,
teaching her a lesson, but there could be no denying
that today he had been as deeply affected as she had.

She still blushed when she thought of how she had
touched him, of how he had touched her, having no
explanation, not even to herself, for the way she had
behaved. No post-mortems, no recriminations, Grant
had said, but what about to herself? Could she simply
forget what had happened between them? She didn't
think so.

Ragtag had once again disappeared, only this time
he seemed to have learned his name, and came when
she called him. But he seemed to want to go again, and
Ryan frowned as he began to bark, forgetting self-
recrimination for the moment. Something was wrong,
Ragtag wanted her to follow him.

She soon discovered why. Lying in the next field
was a dead ewe, and by its side the tiniest little lamb

Ryan had ever seen, looking no more than a few days old at the most.

The ewe was definitely dead, and she had no idea what to do about the lamb. Should she move it, or should she find Grant and bring him back here? She decided the latter would be the wisest, safest course. After all, what did she know about sheep—only that they were woolly and cute!

She told Ragtag to stay with the lamb, and knew by the way he sat down that he had understood her, knew by the apprehension in the little lamb's face that he wouldn't dare move either.

Her lungs felt as if they were bursting by the time she got back to the house, and a frantic search of the yard and stable didn't reveal Grant. She ran breathlessly into the house, asking a startled Shelley for the whereabouts of Grant's study.

He told her. 'But he asked not to be disturbed,' he called after her as she approached the study door.

She could imagine why, knew that the same recriminations that had been going through her mind were probably going through Grant's right now. Well, personal tensions didn't enter into it when an animal's life was at stake.

Grant looked up with a scowl as she burst into the room, making no pretence of working; his desk was clear. 'What do you want?' he rasped.

Ryan allowed herself a moment's sympathy for the strain about his eyes and mouth, knowing he was finding it even more difficult than she was to reconcile himself to the way they had made love. But then she straightened, telling herself once again that this man didn't need her sympathy, for anything. 'There's a sheep—I mean an ewe, and a lamb, and——'

'Calm down, Ryan,' he sighed, his eyes narrowed.

'There are lots of ewes, and even more lambs.'

'Yes, but this one's dead—the ewe, I mean. And the lamb looks—looks sort of lost.'

Grant was already on his feet. 'Take me to it,' he ordered curtly, his expression grim.

Ryan hurried back to the spot where she had left Ragtag and the lamb, breathing a sigh of relief when she saw them both still in the same position, the lamb not seeming to realise its mother was dead as it huddled close against her.

Grant was down on his knees beside them, talking soothingly to the startled lamb, all the time inspecting the mother.

'Why did it die?' Ryan frowned. She could see no visible injuries, the ewe just looked as if it had lain down and died.

He shrugged. 'It's hard to say. Shock, I think.' He swung the protesting lamb up in his arms. 'I'm sorry, little feller, but she's gone,' he said gently.

Tears flooded Ryan's eyes. 'Shock?' she repeated huskily.

'Something frightened her, and very badly.' He looked across the field with narrowed eyes, but the other ewes seemed undisturbed. He turned with a shrug. 'We sometimes get the village dogs coming up here for sport. She probably—Ryan?' he frowned, having noticed her tears for the first time. 'What is it?' he demanded. 'What's wrong?'

She swallowed hard. 'The lamb and I have something in common,' she choked. 'We're both orphans.' She looked up at him challengingly.

'Your parents are both dead?'

'Years ago,' she nodded.

'I'm sorry,' he said abruptly. 'But this little feller won't be an orphan for long, I'll find him a new mother.'

'Like adoption,' she realised dully.

His eyes narrowed. 'Were you adopted too?'

Her head went back. 'No, I was too old. Almost three,' she revealed bitterly. 'Past the cute stage of babyhood.'

'You still seem like a baby to me,' he said harshly. 'Come on, let's get this lamb back to the house.'

Once back at the house Grant carried the lamb over to the Land Rover. 'My manager has the adoption pens near his cottage, so that he can keep an eye on them at all times,' he explained. 'And Ryan——' he turned before getting in behind the wheel.

'Yes?' she frowned.

'Thanks,' he nodded abruptly.

She didn't answer, watching as the Land Rover went down the gravel driveway. How could Grant possibly still see her as a baby after making love to her so passionately?

And she didn't want his thanks for taking him to the lamb. What had he expected her to do, leave it to its own devices? Fresh tears fell for the lamb's loss; she was sure that a replacement mother could never be the same.

She had never really regretted not being adopted herself, she and Diana were very close, and Diana was the only family she had ever wanted or needed.

'You were very good, Ragtag.' She gave him a congratulatory pet, realising that now he was part of her family too. But a very nice part; even after only two days of his company she couldn't remember what it was like without him. 'Let's go and finish our walk,' she suggested softly.

Mandy was once again on her own when Ryan came down for dinner, and her heart constricted at the thought of having to face another meal with Valerie

Chatham. Yesterday it had been bad enough, but after this afternoon she didn't think she could bear to see the other woman touching Grant.

She paled as she realised how much she would hate that, hardly daring to probe *why* she wouldn't like it.

'Grant is dining at Valerie's,' Mandy interrupted her tortuous thoughts. 'He shouldn't be back until late.'

Ryan studiously avoided the other girl's glance. 'I see.' Why did she suddenly feel sick, her palms hot and sweaty?

'He told me about the lamb,' Mandy continued softly.

Her interest quickened. 'Did he manage to find an adoptive mother for it?'

'Don, that's the estate manager, will do it if anyone can. He's very good with the sheep.' Her tone revealed her admiration of the manager.

Now Ryan was totally confused. She had thought Mandy's interest lay in Peter Thornby, now it appeared she liked Grant's manager too.

'I'm glad,' she said woodenly.

Dinner was a strained affair. Ryan hardly touched her food. In fact, she was hardly aware of what she ate. What were Grant and Valerie doing now, were they eating dinner too, or were they in each other's arms? Her sickness returned as she envisaged the other couple making love. She couldn't be falling in love with Grant herself, she just couldn't!

'Ryan?'

She blinked up at Mandy, breathing deeply. 'Yes?'

The other girl chewed her bottom lip, a gesture of insecurity that was totally unlike her. 'I—I came down to the stables earlier,' she said softly.

Ryan stiffened. 'Yes?'

'I called out,' Mandy continued, 'but no one answered.' She hesitated again. 'I know Grant was there because Saladin was out in the yard.'

'Saladin?' Ryan echoed sharply.

'His horse,' Mandy dismissed. 'Ryan——'

'Why are you telling me all this?' Ryan interrupted abruptly. 'Maybe Grant had just been called away for a moment,' she suggested jerkily.

'No,' the other girl shook her head. 'And I'm truly not trying to embarrass you. I know I've been a bitch to you since you arrived, but I'm perfectly sincere about this. I *know* you and Grant were out there, together, but that's really none of my business. I just wanted you to know how vulnerable Grant is, and that if you're really serious about Mark to stay away from Grant. He's already been hurt once, I don't think he could take it again.'

'I—How was he hurt?' Ryan's mouth felt dry, her heart beating erratically.

'Ten years ago he was engaged to be married. He loved Rebecca very much, and she died.'

CHAPTER FIVE

WHEN Mandy told her the cottage was ready to move into the next day Ryan heaved a sigh of relief.

Whether or not Grant had been deliberately ignoring her she didn't know, but she had been deliberately avoiding him. She had heard him arrive home late the previous evening, but with the clean Ragtag already in her bedroom with her she knew there was no chance of a repeat of the night before. Grant was out on the estate all morning; he did not return for lunch either, and it was from the manager that Mandy learnt the cottage was ready.

Ryan couldn't have been more relieved, and she gladly accepted Mandy's offer to drive her to the cottage, the two of them, by tacit agreement, not mentioning Grant.

'Come and use the studio any time,' Mandy offered. 'After all, that's why you're here, isn't it?'

Ryan looked at the other girl sharply, but could see nothing but friendliness in the pretty face. 'Yes, that's why I'm here. I love the cottage!' She looked about her appreciatively.

It was one of the pretty white thatched cottages she had seen on the day she had arrived when she had walked from the station. It was situated about halfway between the village and Montgomery Hall, meaning she wouldn't have too far to walk to get her groceries.

The inside was fully furnished, if a little old-fashioned, having a tiny but fully equipped kitchen, a slightly bigger living-room, two bedrooms and a bathroom upstairs.

'There's no telephone, I'm afraid,' Mandy grimaced. 'But if you need to call anyone you can always use the one up at the house. The fireplace is in full working order if you want to light a fire——'

'In April?' Ryan's eyes widened.

Mandy nodded. 'You'd be surprised how cold it can get in the evenings here. We have central heating at the Hall, so you might not have noticed it. But there's an electric fire stored in the kitchen if you don't feel like lighting the fire.'

'Good,' Ryan smiled. 'I've never had a real fire myself, the flat I share has central heating too.'

Mandy laughed. 'Fires can be very messy. Is there anything else I can do for you?'

She shook her head. 'You've been very kind already. Say—say goodbye to Grant for me.'

'Hardly goodbye, Ryan. You'll probably see him up at the house when you use the studio.'

'Probably,' Ryan agreed lightly, hoping it didn't happen too often. She was as wary of Grant as he probably was of her, having no more wish to get hurt than he did.

She had been stunned by learning of the tragic death of his fiancée in a car crash, and she knew how badly he must have been hurt. But he had Valerie now, and she wasn't stupid enough to think the passionate kisses they had shared had meant anything lasting to him.

Just as they meant nothing to her. She kept telling herself that in the hope that she would eventually believe it. The alternative was too frightening to even think about.

'I'll get back, then,' Mandy said brightly. 'Don't

hesitate to tell me if you need anything.'

How different the other girl was now from when Ryan had first arrived. And she couldn't say she wasn't relieved.

There was only her case to unpack, as she had left the rest of her things in the studio after working in there all morning. She put her things away quickly in the wardrobe and drawers, wanting to get down to the village to buy some groceries before the shop closed. She had been told by Mandy that there was one foodstore, although the food was more expensive than in the supermarkets, but she had expected that.

She must be in better condition than she had been two days ago, for she made the walk in comparative ease, feeling none of the aching leg muscles she had suffered the first day.

After getting her supplies she enquired the way to Peter Thornby's surgery, mindful of his advice about taking Ragtag to see him if he should turn up again.

'Hello there,' Peter greeted her warmly when it was her turn to go in. He looked a little more official today, with his hair neatly combed, and wearing a long white coat. 'He came back, then.' He looked down at Ragtag. 'You've cleaned him up nicely.'

'I think so,' she nodded. 'I had a bit of trouble with him out in the waiting-room, though, he kept growling at the man who came in before us.' She had been surprised by Ragtag's behaviour, she had thought his growls were for Grant alone. She had been wrong, because he was growling at Peter too now.

'Maybe he just didn't like the look of him,' Peter dismissed. 'Animals have likes and dislikes too, you know. He doesn't like me either,' he mused as he tried to lift the dog up on to the examination table and almost got his hand bitten off for his trouble.

'Or Grant,' Ryan frowned, struggling to lift the heavy dog up herself, almost collapsing by the time she had him up on the table.

'Maybe it's just men in general,' Peter shrugged as he quickly carried out his examination. 'He seems in fine health. Good appetite?'

'Oh yes,' she laughed.

'Don't overfeed him,' he warned. 'Hm, he seems in very good health—he's about eighteen months old, I'd say. He needs all his injections, and they're expensive,' he warned.

'I thought they might be,' Ryan nodded. 'Still, if he needs them.' She could always starve for a week or two!

'Someone picking you up?' Peter chatted as he gave the protesting Ragtag his injections.

She shook her head. 'I walked.'

'I'll give you a lift back if you don't mind waiting a few minutes,' he offered. 'I just have to see Mrs White's cat and then I'll be finished.'

Ryan accepted the offer, having bought more shopping than she realised, grateful not to have to carry it back to the cottage. Within ten minutes they were on the road, Ragtag in the back grumbling to himself.

'So the cottage is ready now,' Peter nodded as she told him where she was staying.

'Today,' she smiled. 'I think Mandy was disappointed you didn't come in on Saturday.' She watched him closely.

'Really?' He suddenly seemed distant.

Ryan sensed his withdrawal. So Mandy's interest *was* returned. Then why hadn't the two of them got together?

'I'm sure she'd like it if you called,' Ryan persisted, trying to gauge his reaction. He certainly wasn't as unmoved by this mention of Mandy as he wanted to appear; his jaw was suddenly tight, his smile forced.

'I'm kept pretty busy——'

'Not that busy, surely?'

'Just lately, yes,' he insisted, tightly. 'It's been the lambing season, I'm always in demand then.'

'Of course,' she nodded, wisely deciding not to pursue the subject of Mandy for now. Something had gone sadly wrong between the couple, that much was obvious, and neither of them were willing to talk about it yet. Maybe Grant knew—When did she think she was going to talk to Grant so personally? She hadn't even seen him since that painfully embarrassing time in the stable. 'Come in for coffee or tea?' she invited Peter as they stopped outside the cottage.

'Thanks, I'd like to.' He got out to open the back door for Ragtag, and the dog instantly ran off. 'Will he come back?' he asked with amusement, helping her carry in the heavy shopping.

'Oh yes,' Ryan smiled, confident that he would. Ragtag often wandered off on his own, but he always came back. She had a feeling he was here to stay!

As it was dinner time and she had to cook for herself she offered Peter a meal. After a hesitant refusal she persuaded him to stay, making him relax in the living-room while she went through to the kitchen.

As it was a warm evening she prepared a salad with the lovely roast ham she had bought, putting out fruit and cream for dessert. Not exactly a gastronomic delight, but Peter seemed to enjoy it.

'To tell you the truth,' he confided as he helped her with the washing-up, 'I get sick of cooking for myself.'

Ryan felt very lighthearted, very relaxed. The sun still shone brightly, the back door of the cottage was open so that she could hear the happy chirping of the birds outside, enjoying Peter's company too. All felt good with the world, and as long as she continued not to think of Grant it would stay that way—she hoped.

'No parents?' she enquired softly.

'They've moved down south now that my father's retired.'

'You need a wife,' she teased.

'Don't you start—Sorry,' he muttered. 'Marriage isn't for me,' he amended lightly.

Could Mandy possibly be the other person to tell him he needed a wife, that *she* should be that wife? Mandy had a forthright way of saying exactly what she thought, so it was highly likely that she was the one to say it.

'I believe Grant was going to get married once,' said Ryan with forced casualness, curious about the woman he had been going to marry, although when Mandy had told her about it yesterday she had feigned uninterest.

'Yes,' Peter answered abruptly.

Ryan looked round at him curiously, frowning as she saw how pale he had gone. 'Peter . . .? Did you know Rebecca?'

'Yes.' He was even more abrupt now.

Another touchy subject. The air seemed fraught with them since she had been in Sleaton. So much for a simple country life—London had nothing on the intrigue she was finding in Sleaton!

'Will Ragtag have any ill-effects from his injections?' She changed the subject once again. She seemed to do little else lately!

With all that had been happening since she had come here she had hardly given Alan a thought, in fact, she could barely remember what he looked like, and a month ago she had been heartbroken at their break-up. Once again it was mesmerising green eyes that blocked him from her mind. Who would block Grant from her mind?

'He shouldn't have,' Peter answered briskly, once again the controlled vet. 'Just keep an eye on him. I hardly recognised him as the same dog, by the way.'

Ryan laughed up at him. 'I knew there was an Old English Sheepdog under there somewhere!'

'What a cosy scene of domesticity!' Grant walked in through the open doorway, his mouth twisting mockingly as he dwarfed them. 'Peter,' he nodded curtly to the other man.

'Grant,' Peter returned. 'And washing-up is the least I can do after Ryan gave me dinner.'

'Indeed,' nodded Grant, his sharp gaze on Ryan.

She had no idea what he was doing here, and she wiped her hands nervously down her denim-clad thighs, colour in her cheeks as she saw Grant's gaze follow the movement, vividly remembering how his hands had touched her there yesterday. The look in his eyes, the flare of desire, told that he remembered it too.

'Would you like to join us for coffee?' she offered strongly, willing herself not to be affected by him, but finding him overwhelming in the confines of the small kitchen. 'This place ain't big enough for the three of us!' she did her most ham gangster impression.

'Very good,' Peter laughed. 'And I'm afraid I have to be the one to leave—I have a call to make.'

Ryan swallowed hard. She did not want anyone to leave, she just wanted them to move out of the tiny kitchen. She certainly didn't want to be left alone with Grant—she had no idea what she could say to him.

She chanced a look at him once Peter had left, his

expression still as derisive as when he had come in. 'Coffee?' she asked dejectedly.

'Thanks,' he nodded, leaning back against the kitchen unit, his arms folded across his chest, the dark green shirt fitting tautly across his shoulders, the brown corduroys fitting down snugly on his hips.

Her movements were selfconscious as he watched her, and she wished her hands didn't shake so much. But the last time she had seen this man he had touched her more intimately than any other man had been allowed to.

'I had no idea you and Peter were such good friends,' he said suddenly.

She flushed. 'We aren't. He just happened to give me a lift, so I offered him dinner.' She poured the coffee, then went through to the living-room, aware that Grant had to duck to get through the doorway as he followed her, that his head almost touched the beamed ceiling as he straightened.

He stretched out in one of the armchairs, obviously more comfortable sitting down. 'I think these cottages were built for small people,' he shrugged. 'Is it all right for you?'

'Er—fine!' What on earth was he *doing* here? And how could he act so normally when she felt so uncomfortable? She couldn't believe he had shrugged off their lovemaking so lightly, he had been as aroused as she was at the time.

'Settled in all right?'

'Yes—thank you.'

'Good,' he nodded, staring at her broodingly. 'About yesterday——'

'I thought we weren't going to talk about that,' she said sharply, feeling still too vulnerable about her weakness.

'When you found the lamb,' he finished harshly, his head back.

'Oh!' She swallowed hard at her mistake, and hot colour flooded her cheeks, only to fade again, leaving her pale. 'Is it all right?'

'I thought you might like to come and see it.' He looked at her with cool enquiry.

'Yes, I would,' she nodded eagerly. 'Tomorrow——'

'Now,' he interrupted firmly. 'I'm working through the day, but I have the time now.'

Ryan bit her lower lip; she wanted to see the lamb, but she did not want to spend any more time with Grant than she had to. She had thought now that she had moved into the cottage that she wouldn't have to see him, and she was terrified of the awareness between them, the way she had no defences against his lovemaking. Yesterday had more than proved that—to him as well as herself!

She stood up. 'I'll get my jacket.'

Ragtag wasn't back from his exploration of his new surroundings, so she went alone with Grant, in the Jaguar this time. Grant was very relaxed behind the wheel. He didn't seem to want to talk, and Ryan had nothing to say either. She could hardly believe the short time she had known this man, the way he seemed to occupy most of her thoughts.

He didn't drive to the Hall, but went past it for about a mile before turning the Jaguar into a narrow lane and stopping the car outside a cottage very similar to her own. A middle-aged man came out to greet him, a short man with a lined face, his clothes as casual as Grant's, although slightly more worn, Rex and Riba at his heels, making Ryan glad she hadn't brought Ragtag. Grant had been right about the Labradors, they didn't seem to like Ragtag at all.

'Don Short,' Grant introduced. 'My manager and friend.'

Ryan shook the older man's hand, revising her impression that Mandy was in love with him. She didn't doubt that Mandy did love him, but Grant's method of introduction showed that the other man was a close family friend.

'And you must be Ryan, Mark's friend,' Don smiled, his face rugged, his brown eyes warm and kind.

'Yes,' she acknowledged, aware that Grant had stiffened at her side. Surely he didn't think that because he had kissed her a couple of times she would change her mind about Mark? If he did he was a fool. It might have started out as an act, but Mark was turning out to be as much protection for her as she was for him. How much more formidable Grant would have been if he didn't believe her to be Mark's girlfriend!

'I have to thank you for finding the lamb. He's a lovely little chap, it would have been a shame if he'd perished out there last night,' Don shook his head.

'He would have died?'

'Probably,' Don nodded. 'Come on with me and I'll show him to you,' he smiled.

Ryan looked up uncertainly and saw Grant's nod of approval, although his expression remained grim. He stayed by the cottage with the dogs as she followed Don round to the huge wooden barn at the back of the cottage and went inside with him. Inside were half a dozen or so tiny pens, each one with a ewe and a lamb in them.

'The adoption pens,' she realised excitedly. 'Then you did find a mother for him? Which one is he?' she asked eagerly.

'Over here,' Don smiled.

Ryan knelt down beside the pen, hardly able to believe the tiny lamb sleeping beside the ewe was the same one she had rescued yesterday. 'It's beautiful,' she said in an awed voice.

'Aye,' he nodded, not seeming to find her show of emotion in the least strange. 'He could so easily have gone the same way as his mother.'

Ryan looked up at him, brushing the dust from her knees as she stood up. 'Was it shock?'

'Mm,' he sighed. 'We've had a lot of trouble with dogs this year, and this last week's been the worst.'

'Can nothing be done?' she frowned.

'Shoot them,' came his blunt reply.

'The sheep?' she gasped.

He shook his head. 'The dogs.'

'Oh no!' Ryan recoiled.

'Only way,' he nodded. 'You can't have a sheep-killer in an area like this one.'

'No, I suppose not,' she agreed, secretly shocked by such a drastic measure. But wasn't it just as cruel that the sheep and lambs were killed? She feared she didn't have the hardness of heart for this sort of life. As for sending sheep off to market—she couldn't do it! She was the sort of person who would give each sheep a name, no matter how long it took!

Grant was leaning back against the bottle-green Jaguar when she rejoined him, the dogs already in the back of the car. 'All right?' He quirked one dark brow.

'Yes,' she nodded shyly.

'You see, it can be done.' His voice was husky.

'I think it's a little late for me,' she smiled, understanding him completely, although Don looked baffled by the turn the conversation had taken.

'Probably as far as parents are concerned,' Grant

agreed. 'Although not for a husband.' His voice hardened.

Her expression became withdrawn. 'No,' she acknowledged distantly.

'Thanks, Don,' he nodded to the other man. 'I'm sure Ryan thought I had evil designs on that lamb.'

'Oh no,' she denied instantly, remembering his gentleness with the tiny creature yesterday, 'I didn't think that at all.'

'I should hope not!' Don's mouth quirked. 'I remember that when Grant was a boy he had almost a herd of sheep for himself, he became surrogate mother for so many orphaned lambs.'

Ryan could see Grant wasn't pleased by this disclosure of his childhood. 'Really?' she prompted Don, smiling herself now.

'Aye,' he nodded. 'But even then he had a way with them. He used to get up all hours of the night to feed them, rush home again lunch-time, the same in the evening. It was like that every year,' he shook his head.

'I have more sense now.' Grant's voice was harsh.

Don looked at him, deep respect and love in his eyes. 'I've seen you up all night with a sick ewe, and not so long ago either,' he teased.

Grant gave him an angry scowl. 'If you're trying to convince Ryan I'm human then I'm afraid I'm past redemption in her eyes,' he taunted. 'She thinks my protectiveness of Mark very arrogant.'

She blushed as the older man looked at her curiously, then turned to glare at Grant. He must know that she knew he was *very* human indeed.

Don's eyes narrowed thoughtfully at the high colour in her cheeks. 'I doubt that,' he said slowly, enigmatically.

Grant frowned at him, looking sharply at Ryan, and then away again. 'We'd better be going,' he said tersely, and opened the car door for Ryan, not noticing her almost dazed expression.

She slid into the seat, staring sightlessly ahead of her. It couldn't be true! She wouldn't believe it! A month ago she had thought herself in love with Alan, she couldn't now think herself in love with Grant!

She turned to look at him as he spoke briefly to Don, loving everything about him, the dark sweep of his hair, the mesmerising green eyes, the firmness of his mouth that could reduce her to a trembling mass of wild sensations, the hard body that moved so erotically over hers. She had fallen in love with Grant Montgomery, and Don Short had guessed at the secret she had only just realised herself!

She kept well out of Grant's way for the next two days, not going up to the house until she was sure he was out on the estate, taking a packed lunch with her so that she could eat up in the studio, only leaving when she knew Grant had gone back to work.

It was a conscious avoidance on her part; she did not know how to handle her love for him. She didn't stand a chance of him feeling the same way about her; she knew from Mandy's daily visits up to the studio that Grant was still seeing Valerie in the evenings, and that knowledge filled her with desolation.

She had to be mad, insane, to have fallen in love with such a man. And yet that love was now as much a fundamental part of her as breathing, making a mockery of the infatuation she had felt for Alan. He had been one of the tutors at the college, and had seemed exciting and unattainable. The fact that he had turned out to be very attainable indeed, and had thought she was too, had been the deciding factor in their relationship. With Grant she didn't even stop to question whether or not they should make love, she only knew that she wanted to, that as she lay in bed at night she wished he were beside her.

Such wanton thoughts were new to her, so that she hated to be alone, at a time when she was almost constantly nothing else. She couldn't even lose herself in her work as she had used to, finding she didn't have her usual concentration.

When Grant suddenly walked into the studio late Thursday afternoon her hands began to shake, and she picked up one of her cleaning cloths to cover their trembling.

And all the time she gazed at him angrily, taking in everything about him, from the darkness of his hair, his grim expression, to the leashed power of his body in the dark clothing.

She really did love this man, she acknowledged it even while she feared it.

'Ryan,' he greeted tightly.

'Grant,' she nodded, swallowing hard.

His mouth twisted as he faced her. 'Am I allowed to see the masterpiece?' he taunted.

Ryan flinched as if he had physically hit her. 'It isn't a masterpiece,' she said stiffly, and moved round the easel, giving him no chance to look at her partly finished painting.

'How's it going?' His voice softened, as if he regretted his mockery.

She shrugged. 'Not too badly,' she avoided, knowing she had never worked so slowly, or so laboriously, in her life.

Grant's hands were thrust into his denims pockets, his shoulders hunched over. 'Mandy tells me you've turned down her invitation to join us for dinner this evening,' he said at last.

Wild colour flooded her cheeks. 'Yes,' she confirmed huskily.

'Why?'

'I—Well, because——'

'Mandy seems confused by your refusal,' he bit out at her stumbling effort to find an excuse.

She hung her head, looking at her hands, the gold of her hair dulled to amber in the confines of the single plait down her spine. 'I'm sorry.' Her voice was husky.

'Are you?'

Her head went back at the derision she heard in his voice. 'Yes,' she snapped.

'Then why refuse?' he asked softly.

Ryan touched her lips with the tip of her tongue. 'I didn't come here to be a house-guest.'

'Ryan, are you avoiding me?' His eyes were narrowed as he forced her to meet his gaze, amber lights in the green depths as he probed the blue oceans before him.

She shook her head in denial. 'Why should I do that?' She made her tone light.

'You know why,' he scowled.

'No, I——'

'Yes, damn you!' he rasped. 'The other day I tried to make love to you.'

'Please——'

'And you didn't try to stop me,' he added hardly. 'Ever since then you've been deliberately avoiding me—oh yes, I've been aware of it,' he added as her eyes widened. 'Mandy tells me this isn't the first dinner invitation you've turned down.'

'Not because of you, I can assure you.' Ryan's expression was fierce.

'No?'

'No!'

'I think you're a liar, Ryan. Or do you allow other men to kiss you the way I did, to *touch* you the way I did?' His voice had softened to a caress, the amber flames becoming a fire.

'Not other men, no—only one other man,' she added challengingly. 'I think you know who I mean?'

'Mark!'

His anger didn't please her, but it was her only defence against a situation that was fast moving out of her control. If Grant should kiss her here and now, make love to her, she had no way of stopping him, and she knew she wouldn't want to stop him.

Her silence seemed to damn her in his eyes. 'You miss him?' he demanded tautly.

'Of course.'

'Then you'll be pleased to know that he'll be here on Sunday,' Grant bit out coldly.

Relief flooded through her, though her eyes were suddenly feverish. 'He will?' she said weakly.

'Yes.' Grant spun away from her, glaring angrily out of the window. 'Your reaction tells me you'll be pleased to see him.'

'Of course,' she gasped her surprise.

He glanced round at her, a hard tension about his mouth. 'Did you tell him I kissed you?'

The reason for his own reluctance to see his brother suddenly became apparent! 'The first or second time?' she taunted.

'Either!' he ground out.

'No,' she sighed. 'Look, Grant, I have no wish to come between you and Mark——'

'Don't you?' his eyes glittered. 'It's too late, Ryan,

you *are* irrevocably between us. The sooner you leave here the better!' He slammed out of the room.

Ryan didn't move, but stood there biting her top lip to stop the tears flowing. Grant wanted her away from his home as soon as possible. And she wanted to go, wanted to leave here and never have to see Grant again. But would the pain of loving him go away just by her not seeing him again, would she stop loving him then? She didn't think she would ever stop loving him, even if she never set eyes on him again.

She turned away as the door opened to admit Mandy. The last thing she wanted right now was to talk to the other girl. She wanted to be alone—No, no, she didn't! Oh, she didn't know what she did want any more. Peace of mind, probably. But she doubted she would ever get that again.

'Grant says you still won't join us for dinner,' Mandy spoke tentatively.

'No.' Ryan blew her nose noisily. 'I think I'm coming down with a cold,' she invented.

Mandy nodded. 'It's the change in the temperature.'

For the last two days the weather had been very stormy, although luckily Ryan's roof had held out. 'Probably,' she agreed.

'Did Grant tell you about Mark?' Mandy enquired.

'Yes.'

'Good news, isn't it?'

'Yes.'

'Are you sure you won't join us for dinner?'

'Very sure,' Ryan snapped.

'Is it because of Grant?'

'No!'

'Because I know he's been extra grouchy lately. Maybe he's taken it out on you?' Mandy looked at her anxiously.

'No,' she sighed. 'I've hardly seen him.'

'Oh,' Mandy walked further into the room. 'He's had a lot on his mind.'

'Oh?' Ryan began to clear away, knowing she wouldn't be able to do anything else today.

Mandy shrugged. 'The dogs have been at the sheep again.'

'Oh no!' Ryan was horrified.

'Yes,' the other girl nodded, frowning. 'It's very strange, really, it's only been happening the last week or two. It's probably a stray,' she dismissed. 'I'll go and let you get on with your work. See you tomorrow?'

'Yes,' Ryan nodded, a thought so disturbing bothering her that she didn't even notice the other girl leave.

There was only one stray in the area that she knew of, a stray that she knew from personal experience liked to go off on his own, a stray who had probably only been in the area a matter of weeks. Ragtag!

She tried to tell herself it couldn't be so, she remembered his gentleness with the lamb, and yet she couldn't dismiss it that easily. Ragtag could be the sheep-worrier, and if he was they would shoot him!

CHAPTER SIX

OVER the next few days Ryan kept a careful watch over Ragtag, spending little time at the Hall so that she could keep an eye on the dog. She heard no more about the sheep-worrying, whether it was continuing or if they had caught the culprit, although with the close watch she was keeping on Ragtag, she had a feeling that the latter wouldn't happen.

If it was Ragtag she couldn't believe he was harming the sheep in a vindictive way, she felt sure it was just a game to him. The trouble was, it had turned into a deadly game.

Sunday couldn't come round fast enough for her, and her face lit up excitedly when she saw Mark's red sports car draw up outside the cottage. She ran out to meet him as he climbed out of the low car, launching herself into his arms and hugging him tightly.

'Hey!' He held her away from him, looking down at her with a smile. 'What would Diana say?'

She put her arm through his as they walked into the cottage. 'Has she agreed to marry you? Tea?' she offered.

'Thanks.' He leant back against the kitchen unit. 'And no, she hasn't agreed yet, but I think this three or four days away could be the deciding factor.'

'Absence making the heart grow fonder?' teased Ryan.

'Something like that,' Mark nodded. 'You certainly seem to have missed me?' he quirked one dark brow.

She avoided his gaze, clattering cups noisily on to

97

the saucers. 'Don't be deceived by the welcome,' she said lightly. 'I would have greeted anyone like that, it's been a bit lonely here after living in London.'

'Has the family been rough on you?' he asked softly, not deceived for a moment.

'No,' she answered truthfully. 'Mandy and I have become quite good friends, and I rarely see Grant.' Which was also true; she hadn't seen him at all the last three days, although she had seen his Land Rover a couple of times in the distance.

'So he hasn't been regaling you with more tales of my lurid past?' Mark took a biscuit out of the tin she held out to him.

Ryan carried the tray through to the living-room. 'No, he hasn't. But I hope it is your past?' She sat down.

'Very definitely.' Mark hung back as Ragtag looked up from his place on the hearthrug, growling softly. 'So this is the dog you've acquired. Not very friendly, is he?' He sat down tentatively.

'Actually he is,' she laughed. 'It's just because you're a stranger, he'll get used to you.'

'Ah, but will I get used to him?' Mark continued to watch the dog warily.

Ryan smiled. 'Probably. Now tell me all the news from London. How's Diana? Are Rod and Sally still dating? Is——'

'Here's a letter from Diana.' He took it out of the breast pocket of his shirt. 'I'm sure she'll have answered all your questions. It took her a whole evening to write it!'

'Thanks.' She put the letter aside to read later, not realising how much she had missed the social whirl in London. Here she had too much time to think, to dream, and some of her dreams about Grant had been

Say Hello to Yesterday
Holly Weston had done it all alone.

She had raised her small son and worked her way up to features writer for a major newspaper. Still the bitterness of the the past seven years lingered.

She had been very young when she married Nick Falconer—but old enough to lose her heart completely when he left. Despite her success in her new life, her old one haunted her.

But it was over and done with—until an assignment in Greece brought her face to face with Nick, and all she was trying to forget. . . .

Time of the Temptre.
The game must be played his way!

Rebellion against a cushioned, controlled life had landed Eve Tarrant in Africa. Now only the tough mercenary Wade O'Marc stood between her and possible death in the wild, revolution-torn jungle.

But the real danger was Wode himself—he had made Eve aware of herself as a woman.

"I saved your neck, so you feel you owe me something," Wade said. "But you don't owe me a thing, Eve. Get away from me." She knew she could make him lose his head if she tried. But tha wouldn't solve anything. . . .

Your Romantic Adventure Starts Here.

Born Out of Love
It had to be coincidence!

Charlotte stared at the man through a mist of confusion. It was Logan. An older Logan, of course, but unmistakably the man who had ravaged her emotions and then abandoned her all those years ago.

She ought to feel angry. She ought to feel resentful and cheated. Instead, she was apprehensive—terrified at the complications he could create.

"We are not through, Charlotte," he told her flatly. "I sometimes think we haven't even begun."

Man's World
Kate was finished with love for good.

Kate's new boss, features editor Eliot Holman, might have deva tating charms—but Kate couldn care less, even if it was obvious that he was interested in her.

Everyone, including Eliot, thoug Kate was grieving over the loss her husband, Toby. She kept it a carefully guarded secret just how cruelly Toby had treated her and how terrified she was of trusting men again.

But Eliot refused to leave her alone, which only served to infu ate her. He was no different fror any other man... or was he?

These FOUR free Harlequin Presents novels allow you to enter the world of romance, love and desire. As a member of the Harlequin Home Subscription Plan, you can continue to experience all the moods of love. You'll be inspired by moments so real… so moving… you won't want them to end. So start your own Harlequin Presents adventure by returning the reply card below. DO IT TODAY!

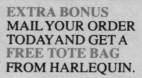

EXTRA BONUS
MAIL YOUR ORDER
TODAY AND GET A
FREE TOTE BAG
FROM HARLEQUIN.

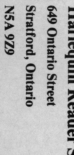

pure fantasy. He had kissed her a few times, was attracted to her, but he didn't even like her.

'So how do you like the country?' Mark interrupted her thoughts.

'Very much,' she surprised herself by saying. 'It has a beauty all its own.'

'But you wouldn't say no to a night out?'

'I would,' she nodded, knowing she couldn't leave Ragtag on his own for long at a time, not in the circumstances.

'Not even dinner?' Mark coaxed.

'Well . . .'

'Join us up at the Hall tonight,' he suggested eagerly.

It wasn't exactly what she had had in mind when she hesitated, envisaging a nice quiet restaurant somewhere, with soft lights and romantic music. 'I don't think so,' she shook her head.

'Oh, go on,' he coaxed. 'I need all the moral support I can get. Grant's sure to start asking questions, and it would look better if you were with me. I can't tell you how grateful I am for your help,' he added seriously. 'As soon as I mentioned Diana to Grant I knew I'd made a mistake, that he would start on his "You're too young to know your own mind" campaign,' he grimaced.

'Perhaps you are,' Ryan put in softly.

'Of course I'm not,' he sighed. 'Grant was going to get married at my age.'

'To Rebecca.'

'Yes,' his eyes widened. 'How did you know?'

Ryan shrugged. 'Mandy mentioned it.'

'You two must be friends! I told you you would like her once you got to know her.'

'Yes,' she smiled.

He nodded. 'Well, Grant was going to marry at twenty-four—the fact that he's never found anyone to measure up to Rebecca is no one's fault but his own. The older he's got the fussier he's got. I'd hate to think Valerie is going to get him through sheer desperation on his part.'

'He doesn't appear desperate,' Ryan derided, remembering the ease with which he had made love to her.

'No,' Mark laughed. 'Still think he's handsome?'

She nodded. 'And arrogant, and autocratic, and cruel——'

'Cruel?' Mark echoed with a frown. 'I've never known Grant to be cruel in his life.'

She blushed. 'Maybe—maybe as a woman I see him differently from how you do.'

'Maybe,' he acknowledged softly, speculatively. 'Please join us for dinner tonight. After all, it would look odd if you didn't on my first night home.'

'All right,' Ryan sighed. 'But just dinner and then home.'

'Deal!' Mark stood up. 'I'll call for you at seven-thirty.' He grimaced. 'I suppose I'd better go and show my face at the Hall now.'

Her eyes widened as she followed him out to the car. 'You mean you haven't been home yet?'

He slid in behind the wheel, dark and bronzed as he grinned up at her. 'It's only right I should call on my girl-friend first.'

'Mark——'

'Mm?' he looked up at her.

'Nothing,' she shook her head. 'I'll see you later,' and she stepped back.

Mark left with a wave of his hand, accelerating down the driveway so fast he left a trail of dust.

Ryan turned and went slowly back into the house, absently assuring Ragtag that all was well again. But was it? She had agreed to go up to the Hall tonight, possibly to spend several hours in Grant's company, and with Mark's astuteness that probably wasn't a good idea. Mark might give the impression of not having a care in the world, but he was after all an artist, with a true artist's ability to read emotion in others—he had more than proved that by his knowledge of the hidden Diana. If he should even guess at her feelings for Grant. . .!

She was ready and waiting when Mark called for her at seven-thirty, ignoring his raised eyebrows at the way her purple dress clung to her, outlining every curve of her slender body. Instead she made much of his own appearance, complimenting him on the dark dinner suit he wore with a snowy white shirt and black velvet bow-tie.

'I have to look the part,' he grinned. 'Valerie expects it.'

'Valerie?' she echoed in dismay, feeling very cramped in the low sports car, with the open roof blowing her hair loosely about her shoulders.

Mark grimaced. 'She's going to be there tonight, with Grant. That goes without saying! I expect to hear the sound of wedding bells very soon—and I don't mean my own!'

She had been hoping that Grant and Valerie wouldn't be at the Hall tonight, but as it was Mark's first day back it was understandable that they were.

After three days of not seeing Grant her heart gave a sickening lurch as soon as she walked into the drawing-room, her hungry gaze fixed on the broadness of his shoulders beneath an emerald-coloured velvet jacket, the lean length of his legs beneath fitted black trousers, his face a coolly polite mask as he enquired what she would like to drink before dinner. Her request for a sherry was made huskily, and her fingers dug into Mark's arm.

'Ouch!' he frowned down at her, misunderstanding her tension. 'Relax,' he encouraged softly. 'They aren't going to eat you.'

His casual reassurance brought back with startling clarity the words Grant had murmured so passionately against her burning flesh, only he hadn't wanted to eat her but *devour* her!

Mark saw her turn pale, and suddenly stood in front of her, shielding her from the others in the room. 'This isn't like you, Ryan,' he frowned. 'What's wrong?'

'Nothing,' her head went back proudly. 'Nothing at all,' she said more strongly. 'Grant has my sherry ready.' She walked over to him confidently, determined not to let him see how he unnerved her. She took the slender glass from him, carefully making sure she made no contact with his fingers, aware of his brooding glance on her, but refusing to even look at him.

She couldn't keep reliving those memories of being in Grant's arms, she had to put it from her mind. Mark was right, this wasn't like her at all, and she couldn't let Grant Montgomery ruin the rest of her life. Their lovemaking had meant nothing to him, in fact she had seen him kissing Valerie Chatham even more passionately after that first evening, and he was still seeing the other woman—still making love to her? Probably. Which was all the more reason for her to behave as if he meant nothing to her.

'Where have you been the last few days?' Grant spoke suddenly at her side.

She looked at him coolly, none of her inner turm[...] reflected in her deep blue eyes. 'Ragtag and I ha[...] been on some long walks,' she shrugged.

'I thought you came here to paint?'

It was as if they were the only two people in the room, Mark, Valerie, Mandy, and the rather pleasant-looking young man who seemed to be her partner, all fading into the background as Ryan's and Grant's glances met and held, sparks of awareness shooting across the short distance between them.

Ryan felt herself sway towards him, felt his hands on her arm, drawing herself away from him as she realised what they were doing. Mark's conversation with Valerie suddenly seemed very loud to her ears, while Mandy's softly spoken partner was flattering her quite shamelessly.

Colour flooded Ryan's cheeks, embarrassment making her voice sharp. 'And to see Mark's home,' she said brittlely. 'We feel that it's important I like it here.'

'Indeed?' Grant's own expression was remote now, the blaze had gone from his eyes. 'And do you like it?'

'Most of it,' she nodded.

'I won't ask which parts you don't like,' he drawled. 'I think that's all too obvious.'

Was he mad? Couldn't he tell how rapidly her heart was beating, couldn't he *hear* it? It sounded so loud to her ears that she felt as if the whole room heard it!

But maybe it was as well that he couldn't guess at her feelings for him, it would simply make a mockery of her claim that she and Mark were to be married soon. Grant wouldn't hesitate in his methods of parting her and Mark if he knew she loved *him*.

'Possibly,' she nodded distantly.

'Darling!' Valerie swayed gracefully to Grant's side,

her brown-eyed gaze razor-sharp as she looked at Ryan. 'You mustn't monopolise Ryan, darling,' she gently reprimanded. 'You'll be making poor Mark jealous.'

'Mark's too sure of me to ever be jealous.' Ryan was the one to answer the taunt.

'How boring to be *so* sure,' Valerie drawled. 'So much more exciting for there to be just the hint of danger about a relationship. But not too much danger,' she added hardly, her eyes narrowed warningly.

She knew, this woman *knew*! And she was telling Ryan that she would allow her relationship with Grant to go so far and no farther. Grant stood silently at her side; didn't he realise what this woman was saying? Or didn't he care? Hadn't he said he wanted no recriminations for desiring her? Heavens, she——

'Everything all right?' Mark joined them, his arm going about Ryan's shoulders.

She was glad of this show of possessiveness, and gave him a dazzling smile. 'Everything is fine,' she said throatily. 'Now that you're here.'

He grinned down at her, obviously enjoying himself immensely. 'I feel the same way.'

'Then perhaps it would have been better if Ryan had stayed in London with you,' Valerie said silkily. 'If you miss each other that badly.'

'I wanted her to see my home,' Mark echoed her own comment. 'I think it's time to go in to dinner now, Grant,' he turned to his brother. 'Shelley has been trying to attract your attention for the last five minutes.'

Grant nodded. 'I'm aware of that,' he said curtly.

'Couldn't drag yourself away from these two lovely ladies, hmm?' Mark teased.

Green eyes bored into him. 'Your taste certainly

seems to have improved.' Grant took hold of Valerie's arm, leading her through to dinner.

'It's working!' Mark said to Ryan with glee. 'You'll have charmed the pants off him by the time you leave here!'

Ryan choked over her sherry, feeling Mark's painful thumps on the back.

'I didn't mean that literally,' he chided as she used a tissue to wipe the tears from her cheeks. 'Or did I?' he added thoughtfully. 'Ryan——'

'I think they're waiting to start dinner,' she told him huskily, not wanting her innermost feelings probed. And Mark was already becoming suspicious!

She kept a low profile during dinner, letting Valerie Chatham do most of the talking, something she seemed quite willing to do, her humour brittle and often spiteful, although no one else seemed to notice that.

There were no brooding looks from Grant this evening, in fact he didn't look at her at all, barely noticing her presence at the table he hosted, seeming intent on bringing out Mandy's partner, Colin Daniels. He was apparently the son of another local land owner, and while he was very pleasant he didn't seem to hold Mandy's attention.

'Mandy seems very quiet this trip,' Mark remarked as he drove Ryan home later that evening. 'Any idea what's troubling her?'

She had a very good idea, but it wasn't up to her to tell Mark his sister was suffering from a painful bout of unrequited love. And just how painful that could be she had found out tonight. The intimacy between Grant and Valerie was even more noticeable tonight, to her at least.

'She's your sister, Mark,' Ryan evaded. 'Why not ask her?'

'Because she'd tell me to mind my own business,' he said ruefully. 'Since she grew up she's seemed to tell me nothing else. I can't understand it, we used to be quite close, in fact we all did. Grant more or less brought us up after our parents died.'

'More lambs,' she said without thinking, blushing as she saw Mark's curious look. 'Don Short told me that when Grant was young he used to take in all the orphaned lambs,' she mumbled.

Mark grinned, 'He's been taking in waifs and strays all his life.'

'He didn't want to take in Ragtag—or me, for that matter,' she grimaced.

'Did you want him to take you in?' he quirked one dark brow.

'No,' she denied curtly.

Mark shrugged. 'What did you think of my great-grandfather's paintings? It's a private collection, you know. Grant occasionally shows them in his gallery, but otherwise they stay on the estate.'

'I haven't seen them,' she had to admit.

'*What?*'

'Look, Mark, I'm your guest. I couldn't ask Grant or Mandy to show me them.'

'Why the hell not?' he scowled.

'Because I couldn't,' she shrugged. 'And mind your language,' she warned teasingly as he began to swear. 'This is your future wife, remember.'

He sighed. 'I'd never be able to handle you! Come up to the house tomorrow and I'll show you the gallery in the house. Some time in the afternoon,' he added. 'I'll be in bed in the morning, country air always has that effect on me.'

Ryan's mouth twisted. 'Don't make excuses,' she taunted. 'We both know you never can get out of bed.'

'Modesty forbids me asking how you could know such a thing!'

Ryan laughed. 'Because of the amount of times you were late for college.' She got out of the car. 'I'll see you tomorrow.'

She had a visitor the next morning, a dejected-looking Mandy, her expression glum as she made herself comfortable in the living-room at Ryan's request.

'What did you think of Colin?' she finally asked.

'Think of him?' Ryan echoed vaguely, having problems of her own, Ragtag paramount in her mind at the moment. He had managed to slip out of the door past her last night as she entered the house, and he hadn't come back until this morning. If he had been at the sheep again ... Heavens, it wouldn't be long before someone caught him if he had!

'Yes, think of him,' Mandy said sharply, sensing her lack of concentration. 'Grant thinks I should marry him'.

'*Marry* him?' Ryan blinked, forgetting about Ragtag for the moment and listening fully to Mandy now. 'Have you known him long?'

'All my life.' The other girl still looked glum.

'You seemed to like him last night.'

'I do like him,' Mandy's eyes flashed deeply hazel, 'but I don't *love* him.'

'No,' Ryan acknowledged softly. 'You love Peter Thornby, don't you?'

'No, I——' Mandy flushed, breaking off her protest. 'Yes, I love him,' she admitted huskily. 'I thought for a while that he loved me too, then—then nothing.'

'What happened?' Ryan prompted.

She shrugged. 'I just don't know. We never actually went out together or anything like that, but the *feeling*

was there. I know it was there,' she said fiercely.
'Then he just stopped calling at the house, except on a
professional basis,' she added bitterly. 'I asked him
what I'd done, why he suddenly didn't like me any
more. And he said—he said I'd imagined it all,' her
voice broke. 'But I didn't, Ryan. I'm sure I didn't!'

So was Ryan. Peter loved Mandy, she was sure of
that. So why didn't he tell her so? She certainly didn't
know him well enough to ask him!

'Grant's convinced I should marry Colin,' Mandy
added miserably.

'Why should you need to marry anyone?' Ryan
frowned. 'You have plenty of time.'

'Grant thinks I need a steadying influence in my
life.'

'He isn't steadying enough?' she scorned.

Mandy gave a rueful smile. 'He thinks not. But
Colin isn't strong enough for me, I'd be able to walk
all over him. Don't look so surprised,' she was smiling
openly now. 'I know myself well enough to realise
what sort of man I should marry, and it isn't Colin.'

'Then tell Grant so.'

'I already have,' Mandy grimaced. 'Why do you think
I wanted to get out of the house this morning?'

'I thought it was to see me,' Ryan teased.

Mandy looked abashed, and suddenly very young.
'It was that too. I thought,' she added mischievously,
'that the advice of an older woman might help.'

'Cheeky madam!' Ryan spluttered with laughter.
'Twenty-one constitutes an older woman?'

Mandy grinned. 'When you're eighteen it does.'

'And I was under the misapprehension that I was
still young!'

Mandy seemed to have emerged from her bad mood
now, and the two of them spent a pleasant enough

morning getting the garden of the cottage into some sort of order. Both of them were exhausted by the time Ryan brought out the jug of fresh lemonade she had been cooling in the refrigerator, collapsing in the garden chair opposite Mandy.

'You're very energetic,' the other girl groaned.

'I've been meaning to do the garden ever since I moved in,' Ryan grinned, sipping her lemonade. 'I just needed some kind soul to come along and help me.'

'I'm glad I was too late to do that.' Mark strolled into the garden and stretched out in another chair. 'But I'll have some of that lemonade,' he grinned, looking very relaxed in white denims and a white shirt.

Ryan made no effort to move. 'You can if you go and get yourself a glass. Oh no, you don't!' she snatched her own glass out of his reach. 'Mandy and I worked hard for this.'

'Spoilsport!' He went into the kitchen, grumbling as he went. 'Am I invited to lunch?' he asked when he came back.

'You both are,' she nodded, 'if you don't mind helping me get it.'

Mandy sat forward, putting her empty glass on the white garden table. 'I'd better get back——'

'Not on our account,' Mark said lazily.

'But you'll want to be alone,' his sister frowned.

'No,' he grinned. 'If you promise to keep your big mouth shut for once I'll let you into a secret. All right, Ryan?' he looked at her anxiously.

'I'd be relieved.' She began to clear away, leaving brother and sister alone together.

'Poor Grant,' Mandy was saying when Ryan came back out to join them. 'He's only trying to do what's best for both of us, as he always has, and neither of us want to go the way he wants us to.'

'If he can choose Valerie as his own future wife he can certainly be wrong about us,' Mark said disgustedly.

'I'm not so sure he has—chosen Valerie, I mean.' Mandy was looking closely at Ryan. 'I'm not sure he's chosen anyone—yet,' she added softly. 'This idea of yours may be benefiting you, Mark, but have you thought that it could be ruining things for Ryan?'

He frowned. 'Who with?'

'Use your head,' his sister said impatiently.

He pursed his lips, starting to shrug. Then he stiffened, looking round at Ryan with disbelieving eyes. 'You don't mean——'

'No, she doesn't,' Ryan snapped. 'Now are we going to have lunch or not?' She glared at both of them, daring either of them to pursue the subject of Grant— because they all knew that was who Mandy was talking about.

Lunch was an uproarious affair, none of them seeming to notice that it was only a chicken salad and fresh fruit. Ryan and Mandy had worked up too much of an appetite to care what they ate, and Ryan knew from experience that Mark would eat anything.

Mandy seemed to have forgotten her misery of this morning as they drove back to the Hall after lunch. The mood between brother and sister was also a lot easier than Ryan gathered it had been of late.

Mark took her upstairs to show her the gallery, throwing the door open with a flourish and letting her go in alone. Ryan was instantly lost in the beauty of Paul Gilbert's art, in the wonder of his paintings, the beautiful Madonna-like women, the countryside that he painted with a poignant beauty of its own, most of them of his beloved Yorkshire, she now realised. Each brush-stroke, the depth of colour, was a masterpiece;

he was a man completely in tune with his art.

'I'll leave you for a while, shall I?' Mark interrupted her absorption.

'Oh—um—Yes, all right,' she nodded absently.

'Join us for tea in the drawing-room when you've finished.'

'Don't you ever think of anything but your stomach?' she taunted.

'Yes—Diana. I'm just going to call her now. I'll give her your love, shall I?' Mark paused at the door.

Ryan nodded. 'And thank her for the letter. I'll be writing back soon.' She once again became absorbed in the paintings about her, Paul Gilberts that she had never known existed.

It awed her to be in the presence of so much exceptional talent. Each painting, about twenty in all, was a thing to be lingered over, drooled over, and she lost all track of time, suddenly realising it was four-thirty and she had told Mark she would join him for tea.

'Just where were you at lunch-time?' Grant could be heard demanding as Ryan descended the stairs. 'With Ryan?' he snapped at Mark's muttered reply. 'Mandy too, I suppose?'

'Yes. But——'

'What's the matter with this family?' Grant demanded angrily. 'I can understand you, but Mandy——! It didn't occur to you, either of you, to let Shelley or myself know of your plans?'

'It was a spur-of-the-moment thing,' Mark answered offhandedly. 'What's the matter, Grant, are you angry because you weren't invited too?'

Ryan gripped the banister and closed her eyes, wishing this were all a terrible dream, but knowing it wasn't. How could Mark say these things!

'What the hell is that supposed to mean?' Grant's voice rose. 'I complain about your lack of common courtesy, and you——'

'I don't think your anger has anything to do with common courtesy.' Mark still spoke calmly; he was obviously not in awe of his older brother.

'And just what does it have to do with?' Grant's voice had lowered ominously.

'I think you're jealous.'

Oh no, Mark, Ryan cried silently. Don't do this to me!

'Of what?' Grant's voice was even icier.

'Mandy tells me you're more than a little interested in Ryan yourself,' Mark taunted.

'Mandy talks too much—and about things she knows nothing about. The fact that I've kissed Ryan a couple of times——'

'You have?' Mark pounced incredulously.

'Yes,' his brother rasped. 'And she responded! What do you think of your precious Ryan now?'

'What do you want me to think?'

'The same as I do,' Grant scorned. 'That Ryan isn't as interested in you as you seem to think she is, that the older, perhaps more wealthy brother, would do as well!'

For a moment there was silence, and Ryan thought Mark had finally been awed by his brother's fury. She felt slightly sick herself. Was that really the construction Grant had put on her weakness towards him?

'I think,' Mark's voice suddenly came out as steely as Grant's had been seconds earlier, 'you aren't fit to be in the same room as a woman like Ryan,' he bit out furiously. 'You may have kissed her, Grant, but you don't *know* her at all. She's the sweetest, kindest, most loyal—Oh, you make me sick!' He was suddenly storming out of the room, coming to an abrupt halt as he saw Ryan frozen on the staircase, her pale cheeks telling their own story. 'Ryan!' he groaned his dismay, coming towards her like a man in a trance.

'What is it now—Oh, no!' Grant stood behind Mark now, his face ashen as he saw the pain in Ryan's bruised blue eyes. 'Did you hear . . .?'

'Of course she heard,' Mark snapped at him. 'Why else do you think she looks sick?' He had reached her side now, concern in his eyes.

'Ryan——'

'Don't come near me,' she told Grant in a cold, controlled voice. 'Mark, I'd like to go back to the cottage now.' She looked at him pleadingly.

'Ryan——'

'You heard her, Grant,' Mark rasped. 'Leave her alone. Haven't you done enough already!'

Ryan never knew afterwards how she got to Mark's car, but suddenly they were back at the cottage and Mark was handing her a cup of very strong tea.

'Drink it,' he instructed as autocratically as his brother would have done. 'Mandy was right, wasn't she?' he added as he watched her drink the hot brew. 'You do care for Grant——'

'No!'

'And he cares for you too.'

'You call that caring?' she scorned, the colour at last coming back into her cheeks.

He nodded. 'Ryan, I think I should tell Grant the truth about us.'

'No!' This time her denial was stronger, and she glared at him.

'But if Grant knows you aren't my girl-friend——'

'He wouldn't have kissed me at all if he hadn't

thought that,' she sighed as she saw his puzzled look. 'It's true, Mark, he only kissed me so that he could tell you about it.'

'Are you sure?'

'He told me so,' she nodded. 'Only I said I would tell you first.' She grimaced. 'Not a very pretty story, is it?'

'Not very,' he frowned. 'But it doesn't sound like Grant at all. He's warned me off girls, plenty of times, but I've never known him to actually try and make love to one of them before.'

'Try is the right word,' Ryan said dryly. 'And he can keep trying, it won't get him anywhere. Don't worry about me, Mark, I can take care of myself.'

But when she thought about it alone later that night she wasn't so sure. She still loved Grant, even after she had heard his opinion of her. Her anger was certainly no defence against loving him.

CHAPTER SEVEN

RYAN saw a lot of Mark the next few days, but nothing of Grant.

'He's gone away on business,' Mark informed her. 'And not before time either,' he added moodily. 'Ryan, we had the biggest argument ever when I got back Monday! If it's any consolation, he regrets what he said about you.'

If he had really regretted it he would have apologised to her himself, not gone off on business somewhere. No, he might regret that she had actually overheard it, but she doubted he regretted saying it.

She took Ragtag down into the village with her on Wednesday morning to get some groceries, putting on the hated collar and lead. She was trying to introduce them to him gradually, knowing that when they got back to London he wouldn't be able to just wander about the streets. Nevertheless, he didn't like the use of them, constantly pulling on the lead, and he had wrapped himself around the concrete post by the time Ryan emerged from the village shop with her bag of groceries.

'You silly boy!' she bent down to untangle him, getting her face licked in the process. 'Anyone would think I'd left you for five hours, not five minutes,' she scolded, finally unwrapping him, then standing up to find her way blocked by a man in ragged clothing, a growth of beard on his face, his hair long and untidy. 'Excuse me,' she made to move past him.

'Oh no, you don't,' the man snarled. 'That's my dog you have there—and I want him back!'

In fact Ragtag had begun to growl now, pulling on his lead—away from the man! 'I think you're mistaken——' Ryan was having trouble controlling Ragtag, almost being pulled over as he tried to get away.

'No, I'm not,' he rasped sneeringly. 'Give him here,' he held out his hand for the lead.

At that moment Ragtag gave one last tug and managed to get free, running off across the fields without a moment's hesitation.

'You did that on purpose!' The man roughly caught hold of Ryan's arms. 'You little bitch!' He began to shake her.

'No, I—I——'

'Duke is my dog—*mine*, do you hear!' he shook her. 'He went off just over a week ago and I've been looking for him ever since. You stole him from me——'

'Is there anything wrong here?'

Ryan turned gratefully at the sound of Grant's voice, not even hesitating as she ran to his side. She hadn't noticed the green Jaguar pulling into the side of the road, or Grant climbing out from behind the wheel, tall and dark in black trousers and a black shirt—and she had never been so pleased to see him in her life!

She clutched at his arm, trembling as she looked back at the angry man. 'I think this—gentleman——' she quivered as she remembered his dirty hands on her, 'I think he's made a mistake.'

'No mistake,' he growled. 'Not on my part anyway.'

Grant looked at the other man with cool green eyes. 'That's enough, Cole,' he rasped. 'Miss Shelton is a guest of mine, and if you have anything to say to her then I think you should say it in front of me.'

The middle-aged man didn't look so aggressive now. He was obviously daunted by Grant's haughtiness. 'I've said all I want to say to her.' His light blue eyes focused on Ryan. 'You haven't heard the last of this!' He turned and shuffled away, his coat old and torn, his trousers ragged.

Ryan was still shaking, offering no resistance as Grant helped her into the passenger seat of the Jaguar, putting her shopping on the back seat before climbing in beside her.

'All right?' He turned to look at her pale face before starting the car.

She swallowed hard, her hands still trembling. 'Yes. Who was that man?'

'Alfred Cole,' he told her grimly, leaving the tiny village now. Alfred Cole was nowhere in sight. 'He lives up in the hills, rarely comes down to the village. It's a pity he did so today,' Grant bit out. 'What was all that about?'

Ryan chewed her bottom lip. If what Alfred Cole said was true, that Ragtag was his dog, would Grant force her to return him to the other man? She had no idea what Grant's reaction would be, she didn't know him that well, even though she loved him. But she wouldn't let Ragtag be made to go back to that *hateful* man. Ragtag obviously disliked him, and if Alfred Cole had been as rough with him as he had with her that wasn't so surprising! She couldn't let Ragtag go to such a man, she just couldn't!

'I don't know,' she evaded. 'He seemed a little— strange,' she understated.

'He is,' Grant nodded grimly. 'He always has been. But he's usually harmless.'

'Don't worry about it,' she dismissed lightly. 'Let's just forget about him.' She turned in her seat to look at him. 'Did you have a good business trip?'

'Who said it was business?'

'I—Mark did.' Colour slowly flooded her cheeks. 'I didn't know it was a secret.'

'It wasn't.'

'Oh.' If he didn't want to talk to her she certainly wasn't going to push the matter!

'I'm sorry, Ryan,' his voice lowered huskily. 'Yes, I had a very good business trip. I have an interest in an art gallery in London.'

'I didn't know that.' Her eyes widened with interest.

He shrugged. 'There's nothing to know. I go up to London about once a month to check up on my investments.'

She remembered now Mark telling her that Grant often displayed the Paul Gilbert paintings—possibly in his own gallery? 'I suppose you're quite good at spotting talent?' she asked. Grant wasn't the sort of man who did things by half measures, if he had an interest in an art gallery then he was an art expert!

'Quite good,' he drawled, glancing at her. 'What's the matter, Ryan—thinking that perhaps my comments the day we met weren't so biased after all?'

'Yes,' she admitted miserably.

'They weren't,' he said without conceit. 'I think art is in the Montgomery blood, probably inherited from our great-grandfather. Mark will be very good one day, once he's lived a little.'

'He's very good now,' she defended.

Grant shook his head. 'Not enough depth. He's been cushioned too much, he needs to feel a little more responsibility for life before he can paint as well as he's able to.'

'Feel a little pain, hmm?' Ryan derided.

'Something like that,' he nodded.

She didn't doubt that he was right; Grant never seemed to be wrong.

'I owe you an apology,' he said suddenly. 'The last time we met I was very rude about you. I had no idea you could hear what I was saying.'

'And if you had?'

He sighed. 'I probably would have said the same thing. You hadn't told Mark I kissed you?'

'Didn't his reaction tell you that?'

'Yes,' Grant derided. 'I think he was more shocked at me than at you.'

'Probably,' she said sharply, opening her car door as they reached the cottage. 'After all, I'm that sort of girl, aren't I?' She got out of the car.

He leant across the seat. 'Ryan——'

'Goodbye, Grant. Thank you for your help with—Mr Cole.' She got her shopping, turning to go into the cottage, closing the door firmly behind her. A couple of seconds later she heard the sound of the Jaguar accelerating away, and knew she could finally relax. That encounter with Alfred Cole had been bad enough, but these last few minutes with Grant had been worse. Why did they have to argue every time they met, and why was she the one who always ended up getting hurt?

She had missed knowing he was around the last couple of days, had even been looking forward to his return, and within a few short minutes that had all been ruined.

There was a soft whining noise at the door, and she hurried to open it, letting in a grateful Ragtag.

Her arms went about his neck as she held him to her. 'I won't let him have you, darling,' she assured him brokenly. 'I won't!'

Her promise seemed easier said than done, and by the next afternoon she was living in a state of tension, sure that Alfred Cole was going to find out where she was staying and come over here and get Ragtag himself.

She did have a visitor that afternoon, only it wasn't Alfred Cole.

'Can I come in?' Grant asked throatily.

Ryan stood back to let him, frowning her puzzlement. His expression was serious, grimly so. Oh dear, he hadn't realised Ragtag could be the sheep-worrier too, had he? His first words seemed to indicate that he did.

'You know why I'm here?' He had refused her invitation to sit down, and stood in front of the unlit fire, a daunting figure in denims and a dark brown shirt.

She bit her bottom lip. 'I—I'm not sure. If it's about Ragtag——'

'It is.'

Ryan ran her hands nervously over her denim-clad thighs, her white cotton top fitting her loosely. 'I—I don't know what to say,' she looked at him pleadingly, 'except that I love him. Surely that counts for something?'

His mouth tightened, a pulse beating in his jaw. 'I'm not a total monster, Ryan, of course it counts for something—with me. Alfred Cole doesn't feel the same compassion.'

She swallowed hard. 'Alfred Cole . . .?'

Grant moved impatiently. 'He came to see me today. I wish to hell you'd told me the dog was his when I asked you what was wrong yesterday!'

He didn't think Ragtag was the sheep-worrier! Relief was quickly followed by apprehension. Ragtag still didn't belong to her. 'Ragtag doesn't like him,' she told Grant desperately. 'He ran away yesterday when he saw him.'

His mouth twisted. 'Can you blame him?'

'No,' she cringed.

'Why did you tell me he was yours?' Grant prompted gently. 'The day you arrived you said he was yours.'

'Because I thought he was a stray who'd adopted me. Peter said he'd never seen him before, and I thought——'

'That if the local vet had never seen him then he didn't belong to anyone,' Grant nodded. 'I doubt if Cole has ever consulted a vet in his life, not even for his stock. So I very much doubt he would bother for a dog.'

'He has *stock*?' Ryan was incredulous.

'He isn't quite the tramp he looks,' Grant drawled. 'He just doesn't see the necessity of wasting his money on things like clothes——'

'—and vet's bills,' she finished hardly. 'Ragtag got his name because of the state he was in when I found him! A man like that doesn't deserve a beautiful dog like Ragtag.'

'I agree,' Grant surprised her by saying. 'But that doesn't change the fact that the dog is his,' he added gently.

'Does he have a licence for him?'

'Do you?'

'I could get one,' she said eagerly.

'So could he.'

'Oh.' She thought for a moment. 'I could buy him!'

'And if Cole doesn't want to sell him?'

'Couldn't you ask him?' Ryan looked at him pleadingly.

'I already have——'

'Oh, Grant!'

'He refused,' he told her softly. 'I'm sorry, Ryan, you have no other choice. You have to give him back.'

'When?'

'Now would be as good a time as any.'

Her bottom lip trembled as she fought to hold on to her control, tears flooding her eyes. 'I—er—he isn't here now,' as she shook her head the tears overflowed. 'He—er—he went out. He—he likes to wander,' she said brokenly.

'I've noticed,' Grant nodded abruptly. 'I've seen him up at the Hall a couple of times. Look, Ryan, I'm sorry. I——'

'You aren't sorry at all!' she shouted at him, the tears flowing freely now. 'You don't like me, you'd do anything you could to hurt me.'

'Ryan——'

'Don't touch me!' She cringed away from him. 'I love Ragtag, and if you take him away from me I'll never forgive you!'

'Ryan!' This time he made a lunge for her, grasping her wrist to pull her hard against his chest, holding her against him. 'I would have done anything not to hurt you,' he murmured into her hair, holding her firmly as she struggled to be free.

'Liar!' She glared up at him fiercely. 'You're enjoying this, I know you are!'

A nerve beat erratically in his hard jaw and his expression was bleak. 'Ryan—darling!' he groaned, and his mouth lowered to capture hers, moving gently against her lips, comfortingly.

'No!' She wrenched away from him, her whole body tense as she glared her anger at him. 'I hate you!' she spat the words out. 'I hate you, do you hear!'

'I hear you,' he said dully. 'I'm sorry, Ryan—I

really am. Whether you believe that or not, it's the truth.'

She was no longer listening to him, was looking in horror towards the doorway as Ragtag strolled in. Go away, you stupid dog, she mentally begged him. But he kept right on coming, sparing a curious glance in Grant's direction, but displaying none of the dislike he usually did.

Ragtag had been right about Grant from the beginning—he was their enemy. He had come here to separate them, and with Ragtag's return he was going to succeed.

Grant had seen him too now, sparing a sympathetic look in Ryan's direction before going down on his haunches to him. 'Come here, boy,' he commanded, and to Ryan's amazement the dog went.

'No!' she cried, rushing forward. 'I won't let you,' she began to pummel on Grant's chest. 'I won't let you!'

He stood up, pinning her arms down at her sides, easily holding her gaze with his own. 'If there were any other way I would take it,' the quietness of his voice held her attention, 'but the dog belongs to Cole.'

Ryan gave a shiver of disgust. 'He's cruel and unfeeling. Ragtag hates him.'

'Yes,' Grant sighed. 'And I can't blame him for that. But Cole is threatening to prosecute you unless you return the dog.'

She bit her bottom lip, feeling the warm flow of blood, but not noticing the pain. 'Can I come with you?' she requested abruptly. 'Can I see where Ragtag is to live?'

Grant pursed his lips in disapproval. 'I don't think——'

'Can I?' she repeated hardly.

He nodded. 'But I warn you, you aren't going to like it.'

Ryan sat in the back of the car with Ragtag, the latter happily in ignorance of their destination, his head resting trustingly on her lap. It was his trust that broke her heart. Ragtag believed her to be his friend, that she would never hurt him, and now she was having to give him back to the man who had instilled in him a distrust of all men—a distrust she was fast learning herself!

Her tears flowed freely as they turned into the yard of a farm, the house old and broken-down, badly in need of a coat of paint, filthy curtains hanging up at the windows. Chickens and other livestock wandered freely about the dirty yard, and Grant's step was careful as he got out of the car.

Ryan cringed back in her seat as Grant opened the car door. 'It's awful,' she choked. 'You can't put Ragtag back in *this*!' Her distress was clearly shown on her face.

'I don't have any choice, Ryan.' Even as Grant spoke Alfred Cole ambled out of the house, dirtier than ever, his smile malevolent as he saw Ragtag.

'Come to your senses, have you?' he sniffed at Ryan. 'With a bit of help from Mr Montgomery, I don't doubt.'

'With a lot of help.' She felt sick, clinging to Ragtag as he pressed back against her.

'He knows the law, does Mr Montgomery,' Alfred Cole leered at her, getting hold of Ragtag's collar to pull him out of the car. 'I've got a nice piece of rope to tie you to until you know who's master,' he scowled down at the dog. 'You'll learn that if it's the last thing I do!'

Grant slammed shut the back door of the car and strode over to the other man to pull him round roughly. What he said to Alfred Cole Ryan couldn't hear, but the other man seemed to pale with each word that was spoken. With a look of disgust Grant came back to the car and slammed his own door forcefully, then started up the engine, his expression grim.

'He won't hurt the dog,' he rasped suddenly. 'I've threatened *him* with physical harm if he does.'

Ryan wasn't listening, but turning to look out of the back window as they drove away, watching as Alfred Cole tied Ragtag to a post by a rope through the collar she had made him wear. He already looked miserable, and Ryan began to sob as though her heart would break. She had only ever loved three things in her life—Diana, Ragtag and Grant—and now Grant had forcibly taken her beloved dog from her. She would never, ever forgive him. Never!

Grant lapsed into silence as she continued to cry, his face grim as he turned to her after parking in front of the cottage. 'Ryan——'

She gave a choked cry and jumped out of the car to run into the cottage, unable to even look at him. She threw herself down on to the sofa, sobbing as if she would never stop.

Half an hour later a knock sounded on the door, but she made no effort to answer it, staring sightlessly up at the ceiling, her arm supporting her head.

'Oh, love!' Mark came down on his haunches beside her, obviously having let himself in. 'Grant told me what had happened.' He touched her shoulder gently.

Her eyes flashed. 'He told you how inhuman he's been? How he's taken—taken Ragtag from me?' Her voice broke emotionally.

'He told me that he had to return the dog to its rightful owner,' Mark's voice reprimanded softly. 'He had no choice, Ryan. The man demanded Duke's——'

'Ragtag,' she insisted fiercely. 'His name is Ragtag!'

'Well, his owner wanted him back, no matter what his name is, or was. The man had the law on his side.'

'And Grant had humanity on his!' she said bitterly. 'Ragtag has gone back to a hovel. And I'm sure Alfred Cole will be cruel to him.'

Mark shook his head. 'Grant will keep a careful eye on him.'

She glared at him. 'When did he suddenly become your best friend?' she scorned.

He gave her a reproachful look. 'I've never denied loving Grant, just as I've never denied respecting him. The fact that I feel I'm old enough to run my own life without his interference has nothing to do with this.'

'No,' Ryan agreed miserably. 'I'm sorry,' she sighed. 'I just—I can't accept what he's done.'

'I understand——'

'I doubt it,' she shook her head.

'But I do, Ryan,' he insisted quietly. 'Against your better judgment you've allowed yourself to become attracted to Grant. Please don't deny it,' he interrupted her protest. 'Your honesty is one of your endearing qualities. And against his better judgment,' he continued dryly, 'Grant has allowed himself to become involved with you too. I don't know whether it's love for him, Grant is too adept at hiding his feelings for me to even guess at that. But whatever the depth of your feelings, you're attracted to each other——'

'You believe a man who was attracted to me could do *this* to me?' she ground out mockingly.

Mark sighed, shaking his head. 'Grant didn't have to come here himself this afternoon, after two days' absence there were plenty of things that needed his more urgent attention on the estate. But Cole threatened to come and take the dog back himself, and I can assure you he would have done it a lot less gently than Grant did. Grant insisted on seeing to the matter himself——'

'Because he wanted to hurt me!'

'So that he could spare you any unnecessary pain,' Mark finished firmly. 'I'm disappointed in you, Ryan, I really am. Grant has never willingly hurt anyone in his life——'

'He's hurt me!'

'Not willingly. Grant suggested maybe you would like to go back to London with me now,' he frowned. 'I think that might be a good idea.'

Ryan sat up, shaking her head; she was very pale and the evidence of tears was still on her cheeks. 'You invited me here for three weeks, I still have just over a week of that time left.'

'Ryan——'

'I'm staying, Mark,' she told him stubbornly. 'I—I have to be here, in case I'm needed.'

'It's no good living on hope, Ryan——'

'I have to stay!'

He stood up, his expression angry, looking very like Grant in that moment. 'I could force you to leave, could withdraw my invitation.'

'Then I'll just find somewhere else to stay!' Her eyes flashed in challenge.

'All right,' he sighed, 'stay. But you're only making it worse for yourself.'

'I'll take that risk,' she said dully.

'I'll say goodbye for now, then,' he muttered. 'If you change your mind——'

'I won't,' she told him stubbornly. 'I'll see you next weekend, Mark, as planned.'

'I—You—Goodbye, Ryan.' His impatience was barely concealed.

The next couple of days took on a dreamlike quality for Ryan. She hadn't realised just how dependent on Ragtag's company she had become, and just knowing he wasn't about the cottage, or happily chasing butterflies—his favourite pastime—gave her a feeling of deep depression. She kept imagining she heard him at the door and would hurry to open it, only to find there was no one there.

It was because she was sure he would come back that she rarely left the cottage. Mandy finally came down to see her, expressing her own regret about Ragtag.

But regret couldn't change the fact that Ragtag was back with that awful man, and when the green Jaguar pulled up outside the cottage on Saturday afternoon Ryan ignored Grant's knock on the door. She had known that wouldn't stop him, and a couple of seconds later he walked into the cottage.

She looked up at him dully, a pale resemblance of herself, hunched over the electric fire despite the warmth of the day.

'Is he here?' came Grant's gentle query.

She frowned. 'Is who here?'

He gave her a narrow-eyed look. 'You wouldn't be deceiving me, would you, Ryan?'

'I probably would if I could,' she told him bitterly, not having seen him since she had left him so abruptly. 'But as I have no idea what you're talking about, no, I'm not.'

He sighed, sitting down in one of the armchairs, stretching his long legs out in front of him. 'Ragtag has run away.'

Her expression brightened eagerly, the blackness

that had engulfed her the last few days suddenly lifting. 'He has?' she said breathlessly.

'Yes,' Grant rasped abruptly. 'I thought he might be here. Cole is convinced that he is,' he grimaced. 'I had a visit from him this morning.'

'When did Ragtag run away?'

'Some time during the night. He apparently chewed through the rope he was tied to.'

'Good for him!'

'Perhaps,' Grant nodded. 'As long as the loose end hasn't got him into trouble. I would have thought he would be back here by now.'

Ryan frowned, realising the sense of what he said. 'You don't think——'

'I've given up thinking where that dog is concerned,' Grant said grimly. 'He's clever enough to lie low until it gets dark.'

'Yes, he is, isn't he?' Ryan agreed happily.

Grant's expression lightened, the tension easing about his mouth. 'I wish I could be angry with you— *and* that darned dog, but I can't.'

Her eyes widened. 'You can't?'

'No,' he smiled, suddenly sobering. 'Although if he does turn up here I shall expect you to tell me.'

'But you know I won't.'

He sighed. 'Yes. I'm sorry all this had to happen, Ryan. But you'll be pleased to know your lamb is doing very well.'

'I know,' she nodded. 'I've been to see him several times,' she explained. 'I call him Samson,' she added.

'Samson?' he almost choked.

'Because he's strong.'

'Of course,' Grant mocked. 'You'd never make a farmer, Ryan, you're too soft-hearted.'

'It's better than being hard-hearted,' she told him pointedly.

He stood up to leave, still in his working clothes. 'I'll call back again tomorrow,' he said abruptly.

'All right,' she nodded, knowing that if Ragtag did turn up here tonight she would make sure he was nowhere in sight tomorrow when Grant called.

'I'll know, Ryan,' he warned, guessing her thoughts with comparative ease.

She swallowed hard. 'You'd do the same thing if you were me,' she defended.

'Yes,' he gently touched her cheek. 'Yes, I would. Until tomorrow, Ryan,' and he moved away from her, although the touch of his hand and the smell of his aftershave lingered long after he had gone.

Ragtag was free! Ryan hugged that thought to her the rest of the afternoon and into the early evening, when she left the cottage door open for his return, standing at the window to watch for him.

By eight o'clock she was really getting worried, re-membering what Grant had said about the possibility of the trailing rope getting entangled in some way. By eight-thirty she set out to look for Ragtag herself, leaving the cottage door open in case he should return while she was gone, following the trail they usually took on their walks together. After all, he might not come back to the cottage, might not return to her at all, might not trust her after she had seemingly abandoned him.

After an hour and a half of looking she gave up calling to him, the fall of darkness making it impossible for her to see where she was going.

As she stumbled into the darkness of the cottage she gave a start of surprise. Ragtag was sitting beside one of the armchairs, Grant sitting in the chair absently stroking his head.

Her eyes widened, and she went down on her knees to cuddle the dog, crying once again, her tears wetting the tangled dirtiness of his fur.

'He's yours, Ryan.' Grant spoke huskily in the darkness.

'I—You—I don't know what you mean?' she choked. 'Alfred Cole——'

'Mr Cole has relinquished all claim to him,' Grant said icily. 'Or should I say he's been forced to relinquish that claim,' he added grimly.

'Ragtag——?'

'Is all right now,' he assured her. 'But another few days with Cole and he might not have been. If you still want the dog, he's yours.'

'You mean it?'

'Yes. He—Ryan!' he gasped as she threw herself at him, knocking him back into the chair. 'Ryan . . .!' he suddenly groaned, turning in the chair to trap her beside him, his mouth covering hers possessively.

Her arms went up about his neck as she pulled him down to her, her mouth opening convulsively to deepen the caress of his lips on hers.

'I've missed you,' Grant moaned into her mouth.

'I've missed you too,' she admitted huskily.

'You have?' He moved back slightly to look at her.

'You must know I have.' Her fingertips trailed lovingly down his hard cheek. 'Oh, Grant . . .!'

'Let me love you, Ryan. Please, let me love you!' His body covered hers as he kissed her with increasing desire, the tautness of his thighs telling her that he was already aroused.

She ached to touch him, smoothing the shirt from his shoulders to touch his bare flesh, her tongue flicking rivulets of pleasure over his body as her mouth moved erotically down, ever down . . .

Grant groaned his pleasure, pulling her to her feet. 'Not here, darling. I like to do my lovemaking in the comfort of a bed, at least.' His arm was about her waist as they slowly walked up the stairs together.

Ryan thought briefly, sadly, of all the other women he must have slept with, and then in the darkness of her bedroom he began to undress her, erasing all those other women from her mind. Grant was the man she loved, it would all be different between them, *she* would make it different.

CHAPTER EIGHT

SHE stood outlined in the moonlight as Grant removed her clothes one by one, first her blouse, then her bra, bending his head to kiss each pert nipple in turn once they had been bared to his avid lips, releasing the catch to her denims to slide them down her hips, coming down on his knees in front of her as she stepped out of them, then gently easing the bikini briefs from her body, pressing his face against her silken flesh as she stood naked before him.

Then his lovemaking began in earnest, as he kissed the tautness of her stomach, knew every inch of her, from her head to her toes, quickly overcoming any lingering inhibitions she might have. She did not even notice the removal of the rest of his clothes as she lay before him, lost in a world where only his caresses mattered, where the only reality was his naked body moving forcefully over hers, aching for their final joining, longing for the fierce thrust of his body as he made her one with him.

'Please, Grant,' she begged as he caressed her inner thigh, drawing her ever near the edge of climactic pleasure and then retreating, allowing her to calm before the onslaught began again. Each time he caressed her differently, gently sucking her nipples until she cried out for mercy, kissing her thighs while his fingertips moved erotically over her breasts and stomach. Always differently, and always drawing back before the final release was hers.

She was going insane with wanting him, couldn't

bear this torture another moment longer, hungry for the glorious surge of passion to merge into a vortex of giving, giving, giving . . .

Suddenly she was controlling him, above him as he lay back with a groan, his eyes almost black as her caresses became as wild as his had been seconds earlier.

His breathing became shallow, and within minutes it was obvious he was far from being as controlled as she had thought he was, his reaction to her kisses and caresses as wildly aroused as her own had been.

'Now, Ryan!' He suddenly stilled her hands on his body, her lips on his hard flesh. 'It has to be now, darling,' he groaned, once again the master, his thighs hard against her as he slowly slid down her body, gently parting her legs to accommodate him.

Ryan never knew afterwards whether she cried out or not, but it didn't really matter, not when pleasure followed so quickly afterwards, when the slow movement of Grant's body within her caused that delicious melting feeling, that submergence to the purely physical, every particle of her being, every tingling sensation of her body belonging to him, only to him.

The sensations were building now, piling in on top of each other, like the crashing of waves upon the sand, and suddenly with a mind-shattering explosion she felt she saw all life's answers, knew herself, knew Grant, knew the very pinnacle of her existence, that she could have died in this moment and want no one to feel a moment's regret.

But it wasn't over yet. Grant taking her through that fire again, joining her this time, quivering against her as pleasure hit every nerve-ending in his body. Neither of them returned to the reality of the world for several minutes, but clung to each other in the wonder of the moment.

Ryan buried her face against Grant's chest as he raised himself up to look at her, shy in that brief moment after passion. Had he known, did he guess that she had given him the gift of her love, of her innocence, that she never wanted anything but him, that he was everything to her?

'Ryan——'

There was a loud hammering on the door downstairs, breaking the spell that had enchanted them, reminding them that there was a world outside themselves, a world determined to intrude, as the knocking was repeated, louder this time, Ragtag beginning to bark at the intruder.

'Are you expecting anyone?' Grant asked gruffly, already standing up. Passion still lingered in the fullness of his mouth, the darkness of eyes that caressed as they touched on her bare shoulders beneath the sheet she had selfconsciously pulled over her.

'No one.' She shook her head, watching him as he moved with lithe grace to look out of the window, frowning heavily as he turned back to her, his naked body beautiful in the moonlight. 'What is it?' she asked anxiously as he hastily began to pull on his clothes.

'Don,' he muttered grimly. 'Something must have happened.' He touched her briefly on the lips. 'I won't be long.'

Ryan didn't care how long he was, knew that she would be waiting. But it must be something important for Don to have come looking for Grant this time of night. And how had the estate manager known where to look for him? Unless his car was parked in the lane next to the house; she had entered the cottage from the opposite direction, and so wouldn't have seen it. What construction would Don put on Grant being here this time of night?

She quickly dressed herself now, hoping Grant had remembered to pick up his shirt from downstairs before opening the door to Don. What had happened between Grant and herself was still too private to openly share with anyone else.

Grant came back up the stairs before she had time to go down. 'I'm sorry, darling,' he picked up his shoes from under the bed where he had kicked them, 'I have to go.'

'What is it? She tentatively touched his shoulder. 'Mandy——'

'No, it's the sheep,' he said grimly, pulling on his shoes.

Ryan paled. 'The dogs again?'

'Dog,' he corrected. 'Don's pretty sure it's only one dog. He even has an idea who it is.' He stood up, pulling her roughly against him. 'I'm sorry about this, my darling. It isn't how I'd envisaged spending the rest of the night.' His expression was longing as he looked towards the rumpled bed. 'But I do have to go,' he said ruefully.

'There's been another attack?' she asked trembling.

'Earlier this evening,' he nodded. 'Several sheep and ewes are dead.'

'Oh no!' Ryan felt sick.

'Don't worry, sweet,' he kissed her softly on the mouth. 'It will be all right. Get some sleep now, and we'll talk tomorrow, hmm?'

'Yes.' She swallowed hard, clutching at his arm as he turned to leave. 'I'm sorry—about the sheep, I mean.'

'It isn't your fault,' he chided. 'Sweet dreams, my darling.' He kissed her hard on the mouth before running down the stairs to join Don.

Ryan moved slowly to sit on the bed. Wasn't it her fault, at least partly? Hadn't she known it could be Ragtag and yet kept quiet about it? Would Grant be quite so loving when Don told him who he suspected was causing the destruction?

She hardly slept, thinking all the time that at any moment Grant was going to come back and tell her it was all Ragtag's fault, that he was the killer.

But he didn't come, and by early morning Ryan was heavy-eyed from lack of sleep, knowing she had to go up to the Hall and find out what was going on, what damage had been done this time.

'Stay here, Ragtag,' she told him once she had fed him. 'Maybe they don't know it's you yet.'

He didn't seem inclined to go anywhere; he was looking very miserable; these last few days with Alfred Cole had obviously been an awful time for him.

It was still early when she got to the Hall, but nevertheless Peter Thornby's Land Rover was parked next to Grant's. Her heart thundered in her chest as she considered the implication of that.

Grant and Peter weren't anywhere to be seen, however, so she went up to the house to see Mandy.

'They drove down to Don's house with him,' Mandy answered her query. 'That's where most of the damage was done.'

'I see.' Ryan frowned worriedly.

Mandy was watching her closely. 'You didn't mind my sending Don down to the cottage last night?' she asked. 'Grant told me he was taking the dog back to you, and when he hadn't returned by the time Don turned up here I thought he'd better come there.'

Wild colour flooded Ryan's cheeks as she avoided Mandy's gaze. Could the other girl possibly realise what had happened between Grant and herself last night? She still wondered at that magic, so she was sure Mandy couldn't know exactly what had happened.

'I'd been out for a walk,' she said jerkily. 'Grant had to wait for me.'

Mandy nodded. 'I bet you were pleased to see him!'

Ryan stiffened. 'I'm always pleased to see your brother——'

'I meant Ragtag,' the other girl interrupted her awkwardly-spoken response.

'Oh!' the colour deepened in her cheeks. 'Yes, I was pleased to see him. I—Grant said I could keep him,' she added.

'Yes,' Mandy nodded. 'Ragtag came back here, I think he was a little confused as to where you were. He was certainly hungry,' she said angrily. 'Grant took one look at him and drove over to see the man Cole himself. He was white by the time he got back, but Ragtag no longer belonged to that horrible man.'

'You mean he just gave Ragtag up?' Ryan didn't believe that for a moment.

'No,' Mandy sighed. 'Grant bought him.'

'*Bought* him?' she gasped.

'Yes,' the other girl confirmed huskily. 'I think he gave him a choice—accept the money and give Ragtag over peacefully, or he could face a court summons and lose the dog anyway. I think Mr Cole decided something was better than nothing, and he took the money. Grant can't stand cruelty, and that man Cole obviously hadn't been feeding Ragtag. He ate two bowls of food while Grant was gone.'

'No wonder he's so sleepy this morning,' she grimaced. 'I gave him another bowlful late last night.'

'He needed it,' Mandy said vehemently. 'There are some people who should be banned from having pets, and Alfred Cole is one of them. But Grant will keep a watch on him in future, and Cole knows that.'

Ryan licked her lips nervously. 'Has—has Grant been at Don's long?'

'About an hour. He wanted Peter to see the sheep.'

'How many were—er—killed?'

'Two ewes and three lambs,' Mandy sighed. 'Grant's very angry about it.'

She could imagine. After all, the estate was run as a business, just as his gallery was, and over the last couple of weeks Grant had lost a lot of stock. But she knew that wouldn't be the reason for his anger, knew the gentleness in him, the warm compassion that would make him feel each sheep's loss personally.

'I think I just heard the Land Rover.' Mandy stood up. 'I'll just check. Yes,' she was looking out of the window, 'it's them. I'll go and see if Peter wants to come in for coffee,' and she hurriedly left the room.

Ryan paced the floor once the other girl had gone, dreading what Grant was about to tell her. If he had proof that it was Ragtag . . .!

The two men were out in the hallway, Mandy having supposedly disappeared to get the coffee. Both men were casually dressed, but Grant towered over the other man, and Ryan's breath caught in her throat as she gazed undisturbed at the man she loved.

She could still remember every vivid detail of last night, those long tapered hands on her body, his lips fevered against her skin, the hard nakedness of his body as——

'He'll have to be destroyed if what Don says is true,'

Grant's grim tone interrupted Ryan's daydreams, the harshness of his voice holding her immobile when she longed to run to him and throw her arms about him, to tell him of the love both of them had seemed afraid to mention last night.

'Yes,' Peter agreed heavily. 'But it won't be easy. You aren't the only one involved——'

'She'll understand,' Grant interrupted firmly. 'I gave her the dog——'

Ryan wasn't listening any more. And she *didn't* understand, she didn't! Had Grant really bought Ragtag for her only to have him destroyed?

She turned and ran out of the open french doors. Grant wouldn't get the chance to take Ragtag. She would take him away now, would get him away from here, to London, where there were no sheep to tempt him.

She missed the bottom step down to the yard, her ankle twisting beneath her on the cobbles as she landed heavily, pain shooting through her as she hit her head as she landed.

She came round to find herself in the back of the Jaguar, her head resting on Mandy's lap, a dull thump in her forehead, her ankle aching abominably.

'Lie still,' Mandy encouraged as she tried to sit up. 'We're taking you to hospital.'

'We . . .?' she echoed weakly.

'Grant is driving us.'

'Grant!' Her eyes opened wide in panic, fighting Mandy's efforts to keep her down, groaning as she sat up.

'What is it?' Grant turned to her briefly, very pale. 'Darling, what's——'

'Don't call me that,' she flinched away from him. 'Don't come near me!' She remembered it all now,

Grant being her lover, Grant callously intending to kill her beloved Ragtag.

'Ryan!' he ground out, very puzzled.

'Leave me alone!' she told him vehemently.

'Ryan, calm down,' Mandy soothed in a shocked voice. 'She's suffering from shock, Grant, she doesn't know what she's saying.'

'Oh yes, I do,' Ryan insisted heatedly. 'I know exactly. I want to get away from here, I want to leave Sleaton——'

'Do you also want Mark?' Grant bit out harshly, his knuckles white as he gripped the steering-wheel.

'Yes,' her eyes were fevered. 'I want him with me, I want him to protect——' As the car went over a bump in the road it jarred her ankle, and the pain was so severe that she passed out once again.

When she regained consciousness this time it was to find herself in a hospital bed in a room on her own, the bright sunshine telling her it was still day, although what the actual time was she had no idea.

'So you're awake, Miss Shelton.' A pretty young nurse came into the room with a vase of flowers. 'From an admirer, I think,' she said coyly, bringing Ryan the card.

There seemed to be a box or something under her bedclothes, making it impossible for her to see her legs, and the panic was evident in her face as she looked up at the other girl.

'Don't worry,' the nurse laughed, handing her the card that came with the flowers. 'We haven't done anything drastic. You've broken your ankle, so you have a plaster on your right leg. We've put a cradle in the bed to keep the weight of the clothes off you.'

She moved her legs tentatively under the bedclothes, the right one feeling very strange.

'That's the plaster.' The nurse straightened the bedclothes around her. 'When the time comes we'll give you some crutches to help you walk.'

Ryan frowned her consternation. 'How do you know what I'm going to say before I even speak?'

The girl stepped back with a laugh; she was young and pretty, about Ryan's age, with lovely auburn hair and mischievous blue eyes. 'They're questions I usually get asked, I just thought I would give you the answers.'

'Maybe you can give me some more. How long have I been here? What time is it? When can I go home? What——'

'Whoa!' the nurse stopped her with a laugh. 'That's enough to be going on with. You've been here, in the ward, about an hour. It's two o'clock. And you can go home when the doctor says you can.'

'Which is?'

The nurse shrugged. 'A couple of days.'

'I can't stay here that long!'

'It's the normal thing to do after a knock on the head and unconsciousness. Shock could set in later. And concussion can be very nasty.'

'I can't stay here,' Ryan said stubbornly. 'I have a dog to look after, and——'

'A young woman came in with you—Mandy, I think her name was. She said you weren't to worry about a thing, that she would take care of everything.'

No, Grant intended doing that, and he would have ample opportunity with her here in hospital. She had to stop him.

'Where's Mandy now?' she asked.

'We insisted that she go home and have some lunch. But we have strict instructions from Mr Montgomery to call him the moment you wake up.' She had obviously seen Grant for herself, a look of dreamy adoration in her face.

'Is there a telephone I could use?' Ryan's voice was sharp.

The nurse moved to one side, revealing a telephone on the side-table of this private room. 'But, Miss Shelton——'

'I'll call Mr Montgomery myself,' she told the nurse firmly. 'And then I intend leaving here.'

'But you can't do that!' the nurse gasped.

'I shall be wanting my clothes,' Ryan insisted determinedly. 'If you could arrange that for me?' She was already dialling the number for the Hall, absently opening the card that came with the flowers. 'Forgive me', it read. There was no signature, but she didn't need one. If Grant had already harmed Ragtag——!

'Miss Shelton——'

'Ah, Shelley,' she spoke into the receiver as the butler answered her call. 'Miss Amanda, please.' She tapped her fingers impatiently against the receiver as she waited for Mandy to come to the telephone, and with an impatient exclamation the nurse left the room. 'Mandy?' Ryan said sharply as the younger girl came on the telephone.

'Ryan!' Mandy exclaimed her surprise. 'I was just on my way back to the hospital. Are you all right? They said you could be out for hours, otherwise I wouldn't have left to have lunch. How do you feel? Are you——'

'Never mind that,' she snapped. 'Is Ragtag all right? Mandy, I have to know!' she choked.

'Of course he's all right.' The other girl sounded puzzled. 'He's here with me now.'

'He—he is?'

'Of course. He's eating us out of house and home,' she added dryly.

That sounded like the Ragtag she knew and loved. 'Grant hasn't—said anything?'

'No.' Mandy was suddenly serious. 'Ryan, what's happened between you two? This morning Grant seemed—elated. I thought—I thought it was because the two of you had—sorted out your difficulties.'

'Don't be polite, Mandy,' she said sharply. 'You thought we'd done more than that.'

'No, I didn't,' Mandy protested, but Ryan could hear the lack of conviction in her voice.

'You did,' she sighed. 'But that's irrelevant now. Whatever—happened was a mistake, one we both realise——'

'Not Grant——'

'Oh yes, him too. Mandy, I want you to take care of Ragtag until I get there. Will you do that?'

'You know I will. But, Ryan——'

'I'll be there in about an hour——'

'Oh no, you won't, young lady!' The telephone was plucked out of her hand and the doctor spoke firmly into the receiver. 'Miss Shelton will not be going anywhere, not today or tomorrow, and possibly not even the day after.'

'Give me that,' Ryan demanded, and sat up, only to crumple back against the pillows, as everything crashed in on her, the whole world seeming to rest on her temples.

For the next thirty-six hours she knew nothing, although the doctor told her afterwards that the concussion had been quite mild in the circumstances.

It didn't feel mild to her, and she woke up with a raging thirst, and a headache that seemed to be a permanent throb in her temple. Mandy sat beside her bed, instantly putting down her magazine when she saw Ryan was awake.

'Ragtag?' she managed to groan between parched lips.

'I don't believe it! For goodness' sake, Ryan,' Mandy sighed impatiently. 'You've been delirious for almost two days and you wake up and ask about your dog!'

'Well?'

'He's fine, missing you a little I think, but otherwise he's well. Now how are you? Grant's been out of his mind——'

'I don't want to talk about Grant.' She turned away. 'If he's been concerned it's only because my accident happened while I was at the Hall.'

'I'll get the doctor.' Mandy stood up. 'We don't want you to collapse again.'

'By all means get the doctor,' Ryan nodded, too weak to argue any more. 'But I don't want to see Grant. You understand, Mandy?'

'I understand what you're saying,' Mandy sighed. 'But I don't know why you're saying it.'

'You'll keep Ragtag—safe for me?'

'I said I would——'

'Promise me!'

'All right, I promise,' Mandy nodded impatiently. 'I can't understand why you keep fussing about him. He's perfectly all right. Now just lie there until I get the doctor. Mark's at the Hall, by the way,' she paused at the door, 'and he has Diana with him. The four of us have been taking it in turns to sit with you,' she explained. 'I'll call him as soon as I've spoken to the doctor.'

Ryan saw a lot of Mandy, Mark and Diana the next few days, but, at her request, nothing of Grant. No one questioned her further about that, perhaps putting it down to the fact that she had been ill, and when it came time for her to go home it was Mark and Diana who drove her—in Grant's Jaguar.

'I'll stay in the cottage with you until you're ready to go back to London,' Diana told her, a small pretty girl with black curly hair and warm brown eyes.

'I'm ready now,' she said dryly, her right leg stretched out on the back seat of the car, her crutches in the boot.

'You look it,' Diana grimaced. 'And to think none of this would have happened if this stupid idiot,' she punched Mark in the arm, 'hadn't persuaded you to pretend to be his girl-friend. I just may never forgive him!'

'You'd better, you're going to marry me,' he mocked.

'I haven't decided yet. This stupid antic may change my mind,' said Diana with pretended hauteur.

'If you'd ever made it up in the first place,' he grimaced, still waiting for an answer to his proposal of marriage.

'I'm glad I didn't now.' She gave him a disgusted look. 'What a stupid idea!'

'Ryan agreed to it. Besides, it worked, didn't it?'

Diana sighed. 'I would hardly say that. Poor Ryan has had to put up with your brother's rudeness, she's got herself a dog that seems to have caused her nothing but trouble, partially adopted a lamb, and now she's broken her ankle. You have a lot to answer for, Mark.'

'I didn't make her stay——'

'You didn't exactly make it easy for her to leave. I think——'

'When the two of you have quite finished!' Ryan laughed. 'I'm adult enough to make my own decisions, and my own mistakes.' Diana had left one thing out of the list of disasters that had befallen her since she came here, the one that hurt most of all. She loved Grant, he was her lover, and it was all over between them.

After three days Ryan was very competent on the crutches she had at first cursed, could manage to get about quite confidently. As Mandy had told her Ragtag was in fine health, ecstatic about having her back at the cottage, although she wasn't confident enough on the crutches to take him for the long walks they used to enjoy together.

Mark was a constant visitor, and Ryan could see the love he and Diana had for each other deepening every day. Of Grant she saw nothing, and her life settled down to a sort of peace. She spent most of her time out in the garden, just longing for the time she could return to London.

The doctor finally gave his permission for her to travel, and with only two days to go to the weekend Mark decided they could all leave on Saturday.

'Why don't you put him out of his misery?' Ryan teased Diana as the other girl prepared for her luncheon date with him. 'Tell him you'll marry him.'

Diana smiled. 'Not yet. I think he deserves to suffer a little for what he got you involved in. How about you, Ryan?' she sobered. 'Are you going to see Grant before you leave?'

Her expression was suddenly blank, the teasing gone from her eyes, no longer smiling. 'Why should I want to see him?'

'Ryan——'

'I sent him a note thanking him for my flowers,' she dismissed.

'Forgive me,' he had said. And she knew she never

would. The man she loved had had compassion and love, and the hard ruthless side of Grant she could never accept. The fact that Ragtag was still alive and well she put down to Grant's guilt, knew that if they stayed here it would only be a matter of time before he once again revealed that part of his nature which she could never love, the part that destroyed.

'Ryan,' Diana spoke slowly, 'I haven't mentioned this earlier because Mark didn't think I should, but he says there's something between you and Grant——'

'He's wrong,' Ryan said stiffly, now knowing the reason no one had mentioned Grant to her. They all knew that she had loved him.

'There *was* something,' Diana insisted firmly. 'This is me, love,' she added gently. 'And I know you, maybe better than anyone else. You've changed since you've been here. You used to be carefree and outgoing, now it takes all our efforts to get you to talk. And Grant is so grim! Nice, but grim. And Mark says he isn't usually as bad as that.'

'A couple of weeks ago he thought he was an ogre.' Ryan's mouth twisted.

'He didn't, not really. He's always admired Grant, I think he just resents his domination sometimes.' She grimaced. 'Wait until we're married, I'll show him what domination is!'

The two girls were still laughing when Mark arrived, although Ryan's humour faded as soon as the other couple left for their pub lunch, she having refused to join them. She still tired easily on her crutches, besides which, she wasn't very good company at the moment. As Diana said, she spoke little nowadays. She had nothing to say, and only wanted to get away from Grant and back to the safe world she had in London.

She had drifted off to sleep out in the garden, her plastered foot resting on a stool, when a rather persistent fly kept landing on her nose. She brushed it away several times, then finally sat up, her eyes opening wide as she saw the man who sat next to her.

'Hi,' Grant greeted her huskily, the long piece of grass he had been tickling her nose with still in his hand.

She was instantly alert, sitting ramrod-straight in her chair. Grant looked leaner than she remembered, a little strained about the eyes, and for a few brief seconds she wondered if he were missing the closeness they had achieved as much as she was. Then she dismissed the idea. If Grant looked strained it was because of worry about the estate; it certainly had nothing to do with her.

'I received your letter,' he told her softly.

'Yes.' She stared woodenly ahead of her, knowing his gaze never left her.

'We have to talk——'

'We don't *have* to do anything, Grant!' Her eyes flashed. 'I would have thought I made it perfectly obvious the last few days that I have nothing to say to you, either now or in the future.'

'Is that why you signed your note so formally, Ryan Shelton?' he rasped.

She nodded. 'And why it was addressed to Mr Montgomery.'

'What happened, Ryan?' He grasped her hand. 'Somewhere between Thursday night—that beautiful night,' his voice was husky with emotion, 'and Friday morning, you'd grown to hate me.'

'Not hate, Grant.' She withdrew her hand with an effort. 'I saw the situation for what it was——'

'I wish to blazes I did!' he said harshly. 'Ryan, that

time together was beautiful, why are you throwing it away?' His eyes were narrowed to puzzled green pools.

How she wished she could get up and walk away, but this damned ankle stopped even that dignity. Instead she had to sit here and suffer through this embarrassment, while Grant attempted to probe her deepest emotions. But he wouldn't know of her love, she would do anything, say anything to prevent that.

She looked at him with steady blue eyes. 'I'm not throwing anything away, there was nothing to throw away.'

'I made love to you,' he ground out. 'You made love to me! I know you more intimately than any other man!'

She couldn't prevent the hot colour flooding her cheeks. 'Does that mean we have to have a post-mortem about it?' she snapped.

Grant had no restrictions. He got up to pace the garden, his hands thrust into his trousers pockets. 'It isn't a post-mortem, Ryan,' he looked at her with hurt eyes. 'Heaven knows I don't want to embarrass you——'

'Then don't!' Ryan looked down at her hands. Grant might know her more intimately than any other man, but she knew him too, knew every hard, muscled plane of his body, had touched the silkiness of his skin, knew the caresses he liked, knew how to touch him in a way that drove his desire into a frenzy. How could she not be embarrassed when he insisted on talking about it so intimately! 'We made love once. It was a mistake.'

'I don't believe that——'

'I was grateful—the situation got out of hand,' she said heatedly.

'Grateful?' he repeated softly, dangerously so. 'For what?'

'For bringing Ragtag back to me——'

'You don't make love with a man for a reason like that!'

'I did!' she almost shouted at him.

'You were a virgin——'

'No!' She paled.

'You were, damn you!' Grant glared down at her fiercely. 'I have enough experience to know something like that.'

'You're wrong,' she told him coldly. 'And I'm sure Mark could verify that—if you were ungentlemanly enough to ask him.'

Their gazes locked and held, Grant's anger a tangible thing. At last he sighed. 'I didn't come here today to upset you——'

'Why did you come?' Her agitation was obvious now. 'Did you hope Mark would be here so that you could tell him I'd slept with you?'

'You know that isn't true!' There was a white ring of tension about his mouth. 'What happened between us is—private. Unless you've told him?' His eyes narrowed.

'I'm not that proud of it!' Ryan's mouth twisted.

'And you think I am?' he groaned. 'You were going to marry my brother——'

'Were?' she echoed sharply, sensing a way of alienating Grant for ever. 'What makes you think I'm still not?'

He seemed to go even paler, if that were possible. 'You still mean to marry Mark? Even after——'

'Did you think I wouldn't?' she scorned.

'You want to become my *sister-in-law*?'

'It hasn't gone as far as that yet, but I do want you to realise that what happened the other night between us didn't change my feelings for Mark. I'm sorry if you thought there was more to it than there actually was, but this is the permissive society, Grant. You no longer have to be in love with someone to sleep with them. You enjoyed it, didn't you?'

'You know I did,' he muttered.

'And so did I. Now let's forget about it,' she dismissed.

'I can't,' he shook his head.

'So you intend telling Mark?'

'No,' he said tautly, 'of course not. I just—I can't believe that will never happen again,' he groaned, his eyes tortured.

Ryan's shrug was deliberately nonchalant. 'If you feel that strongly about it I don't see why it shouldn't. When I'm Mark's wife we're sure to see a lot of each other. I'm sure Mark won't be around all the time,' she added provocatively.

Grant swallowed hard, a disbelieving look of disgust on his face. 'You think——' he took a steadying breath. 'You think I could have an affair with my brother's wife?'

'Why not?' she looked at him innocently. 'You made love to your brother's girl-friend.'

'That was different——'

'Was it?' she scorned. 'Why?'

'We're both free, not legally committed to anyone. If—When you marry Mark you'll become a member of my family, forbidden to my bed.'

Ryan shrugged. 'It will be your loss. I'm sure Mark won't be possessive—neither of us are. He's gone out to lunch with Diana today, and I don't mind at all.'

'Diana is the same girl I warned you about when you first arrived here?'

'Yes.'

'Your own flatmate?'

'Why not?' She could see he was hating this, knew that this attitude was alienating him completely, that he was slowly coming to hate her.

That was better than knowing he still wanted her! One thing seeing him again today had done, and that was show her that his callousness about Ragtag might have hurt her, but that her love for him was still very much alive. It had no right to be, and she hated herself for her weakness, but she knew that if Grant still wanted her, that if he made love to her, she would respond as lovingly as she had before.

He shook his head. 'This doesn't sound like you, Ryan——'

'And just what do you really know about me?' she interrupted sharply. 'I was someone you desired, someone you wanted. Well, now you've had me, so where do you want to go from here? I offered to continue sleeping with you, but you said no, so what *do* you want?'

His eyes narrowed. 'You aren't making sense, Ryan,' he frowned. 'If you wanted to continue the affair why did you refuse to see me at the hospital?'

Drat, she had forgotten that! 'Even we liberated girls can have a guilty conscience,' she invented lightly. 'But seeing Mark again has shown me I have no need to feel that way. Maybe I should write you another note, this time addressed to "my darling Grant". Would you like that?' she teased flirtatiously.

'No, I wouldn't,' he snapped harshly, shaking his head. 'I've been wrong about you—I'm sorry I troubled you.' He turned on his heel and walked away, the sound of the Jaguar leaving a couple of seconds later.

Ryan lay back in her chair with her eyes closed. What a performance! Laurence Olivier would have been proud of her.

But she wasn't proud of herself! She had deliberately made herself out to be one of the modern girls she most despised, the sort that took what love and affection they could from sharing a man's bed, only to find themselves immediately discarded.

And Grant had discarded her now, she knew that. He didn't like the girl she had pretended to be, just as she hadn't. Why didn't she just tell him that she couldn't bear the pain of loving a man without a heart, a man who had become hardened to death and killing? Because she still couldn't quite admit to herself that Grant was that man!

She cried then, cried for the love that wouldn't die, the love she doubted would ever die.

But she would save her beloved Ragtag, would take him away from here, away from the temptation that threatened his life—and away from the temptation that threatened hers too.

But it seemed her misery wasn't over for one day, that fate could be even crueller. Another car was coming down the narrow lane to the cottage, not Mark's, she knew the sound of his sports car off by heart.

The sight of the yellow Porsche made her groan. Valerie Chatham! She hadn't seen the other woman for a couple of weeks now, hadn't particularly cared whether or not she ever saw her again, and she knew the dislike was mutual.

This woman had never paid a friendly visit on anyone in her life, Ryan was sure of that, and she had no idea what she could want here now.

CHAPTER NINE

VALERIE slid gracefully out of her seat, the purple suit she wore clinging to the perfection of her body, a pillbox hat in the same purple shade perfect against the darkness of her hair.

She swayed smoothly over to where Ryan sat, her high heels clicking on the concrete pathway. 'How pale you look,' was her opening comment as she sank silkily into one of the chairs, looking in the best of health herself, her skin a glowing gold.

'I'm always pale,' Ryan said without rancour, not willing to show her resentment to this woman. She hadn't regretted not seeing this woman the last couple of weeks, and the sooner she left the better Ryan would feel.

'Yes,' Valerie drawled. 'So clumsy of you to fall over like that.'

Ryan's eyes widened at this frontal attack. 'I can assure you I didn't do it on purpose!'

Valerie looked at her coldly. 'Didn't you?' Her gaze was insolent. 'It had the desired effect, didn't it?'

'Did it?'

'Oh yes,' the other woman gave a hard laugh. 'Poor Grant felt it was his responsibility to take care of you. And, of course, the way you threw yourself at him didn't help the situation. The poor man has been quite guilt-stricken about that too.'

Ryan was still with indignation now. 'Really?' Surely Grant hadn't discussed her with this woman, told her they had made love? If he had it didn't fit in with the things he had said to her a little over an hour ago. Could Valerie Chatham possibly be playing a grand bluff?

'You're so young,' Valerie scorned now. 'You don't have the faintest idea how to keep a man like Grant.'

'And you do?'

'Certainly. He wanted you, I let him have you. Now he's come back to me.'

'Suitably penitent, I hope?' Ryan taunted, more sure of herself now.

Brown eyes flashed Valerie's dislike, although she quickly had herself under control again, smiling falsely. 'Grant and I have been lovers a long time, we have no need to make apologies for light flirtations, we can be civilised about these things. When I marry Grant——'

'I thought it was "if",' Ryan mocked.

'Did you?' Arched eyebrows rose, and Valerie smoothed the silky skirt of her suit down her slender thighs. 'I can assure you it will be when. And once we're married Grant won't even look at you.'

'Maybe I don't want him to!' Ryan was tiring of this game, didn't believe for a moment that this woman had any real authority to talk of marrying Grant. He was above all honest, and he had told her only minutes ago that he was morally free, not legally committed to anyone. And that included Valerie Chatham!

Valerie's mouth twisted. 'You've been a little too obvious in your interest in him, my dear. I remember Grant was quite embarrassed at first—and then he thought it might be amusing to flirt with Mark's little girl-friend. But I doubt if you considered it a flirtation, did you, Ryan?'

'I have no idea what you're talking about—Valerie,' Ryan taunted. 'If you're so sure of Grant why come and see me? I can't hurt you, surely?'

'Of course you can't,' the other woman said waspishly. 'I'm just trying to point out to you how awkward it could be for you if you insist on pursuing Grant in this way when we're married.'

'Oh, I don't think so.' Ryan looked at her in challenge. 'You see, Grant and I have already sorted this matter out.'

Valerie tried to hide her surprise, but she didn't do a very good job of it; there was a flush to her cheeks and her eyes narrowed. 'Indeed?' she snapped.

'Mm,' Ryan nodded. 'We see no reason to stop our affair.'

'Affair——?' the other woman spluttered, completely disconcerted now.

Ryan looked at her coolly. She had called this woman's bluff, and she knew she had won. 'Maybe you should go back and talk to Grant,' she advised haughtily. 'It would appear he hasn't been telling you everything after all.'

'You little——'

'Please—Valerie,' drawled Ryan. 'Remember, we're civilised people.'

'You're an opportunist little bitch!' Valerie stood up, no longer trying to hide her anger behind a veneer of sophistication. 'You think you can have both Grant and Mark?'

'And can't I?'

The brown eyes glittered her hatred. 'Not if I have anything to do with it!'

'And do you?' Ryan mocked, wishing the other woman would just leave.

'Oh yes!' Valerie was breathing heavily, her chest rising and falling in her agitation. 'Once I've told Grant about this conversation——'

'Is that a good idea?'

Triumph shone in the other woman's eyes. 'So you aren't so confident after all.'

'I was thinking of you,' Ryan told her calmly. 'I've merely related to you the plans Grant and I have made for the future. But I'm sure Grant would be interested in your side of this conversation. After all, he's already heard mine.'

'You—you——'

Ryan watched as Valerie went from being supremely confident to outrageously angry. And considering the context of the conversation Ryan considered *she* was the one who should be angry—furiously so. Valerie might have guessed at a lot of the relationship between Grant and herself, but she hadn't necessarily guessed at all of it.

'He's mine,' Valerie hissed. 'He has been for the last year, and he will be again when you've gone.'

Ryan shrugged. 'As I said, I think Grant is the one you should be talking to.'

'Oh, I intend to,' Valerie spat out, all trace of beauty gone in her fury. 'We'll see which of us stays in Grant's life!' She turned and walked back to her car, no longer the composed woman who had arrived fifteen minutes earlier.

Ryan relaxed with a sigh as the other woman drove away. Valerie Chatham might not realise it yet, but it was a no-contest as far as Grant was concerned—she didn't even want to fight for him.

But the other woman's visit had unnerved her, and her hand was shaking slightly as she poured herself some orange juice. It was one thing to face a rival on equal terms, quite another to face them when you couldn't even get up and walk away when you wanted to. And several times during that conversation she had wanted to.

'What did she want?'

Ryan looked up to find Mark blocking out the sun. 'Sorry?' she blinked, having been so deep in thought she hadn't even noticed Mark and Diana's return.

'Valerie,' he lounged next to her. 'What did she want?'

'Why, to enquire after my health, of course,' she drawled.

Diana was frowning. 'She looked furious. She almost drove Mark and me off the road at the end of the lane,' she grimaced.

'And she wasn't enquiring after your health,' Mark said dryly. 'Not unless she was asking when the funeral is.'

Ryan's mouth quirked at his humour. 'Not quite,' she smiled. 'But close. She was warning me off Grant—I think. I'm not sure she really knew why she was here herself.'

'Stupid woman!' Mark scowled. 'If Grant gets to hear about this he'll be furious.'

'But he isn't going to hear about it—is he?' she said pointedly.

'If you say not,' he shrugged.

'I do.'

'Okay,' he sighed. 'Although I think you should know Grant hasn't seen Valerie for over a week now. When I asked him about it he almost bit my head off.'

'Maybe they've argued,' she dismissed uninterestedly.

'Ryan——'

'Did you have a nice lunch?' she pointedly changed the subject. 'And are wedding bells ringing yet?'

Luckily, for her sake, they weren't, but she knew it wouldn't be much longer before Diana accepted Mark's proposal. And when it happened she would be happy for both of them—she just hoped it wouldn't happen until they had all returned to London and they were far away from Grant!

On the eve of their departure back to London she and Diana were invited up to the Hall for dinner. Ryan didn't really want to go, but she could hardly refuse without being extremely rude.

'You look lovely,' Diana assured her.

She did feel quite attractive in a black dress, its long length hiding the clumsiness of her plastered ankle.

'No crutches for you tonight.' Mark put them aside, sensing her reluctance to use them. 'Tonight I'll be your mobility.' He swept her up in his arms. 'Your carriage awaits without, milady,' he added teasingly.

'Sometimes I think you're without,' Diana said dryly as she followed behind them. 'Without brains.' She slid into the passenger seat of the Jaguar while Mark settled Ryan in the back.

'And that's before we're married!' Mark groaned, getting in behind the wheel. 'I dread to think what insults I shall get once we're husband and wife.'

'Wife and husband,' Diana told him. 'Let's get our priorities right.'

Ryan felt ridiculous being carried into the Hall, and the three of them were in hysterics as Mark almost dropped her.

'Let me.'

'What——? Oh, Grant,' Mark grinned as he turned to his brother, relinquishing Ryan without a murmur. 'The cavalry are here!'

Ryan could quite cheerfully have hit him! How dared he just hand her over to Grant like this!

She couldn't even look up at Grant, her eyes on a level with his chin, his jaw rigid. And he smelt of the tangy aftershave she had detected on her own skin each time he had kissed her, the masculine odour stirring her senses.

He carried her through to the lounge with ease, seeming no more inclined to talk than she was, putting her down on the sofa to step back. She chanced a glance at him, at once wishing she hadn't, as Mark and Diana's lighthearted chatter faded into the background, her hungry gaze devouring him.

He looked more strained than ever, his skin very pale, his loss of weight more noticeable. And if she were staring at him he was staring straight back, and her cheeks became flushed as he seemed unable to look away.

'How is your ankle?' he asked huskily, also seeming to have forgotten the other couple.

'Very well—thank you. Well enough to travel back with Mark tomorrow.'

Grant nodded. 'He told me.'

'I—I think it's best, don't you?' She swallowed hard. This meeting was being as difficult as she had thought it would be.

'For whom?' he said gruffly.

'Well, I—It means Ragtag and I will be away from here. All your worries will be over.'

'Will they?' he sighed.

'Of course they will,' she insisted briskly. 'But if there's any way I can compensate——'

'Compensate!' he rasped. 'How the hell could you do that?' His eyes glittered with anger.

'Well, I——'

'No, you can't *compensate*, Ryan,' he bit out harshly. 'We'll just count the incident as over, shall we?'

'If you're sure . . .'

'Very,' he turned away abruptly. 'Perhaps I can

offer you a drink before dinner?' His voice was silkily charming as he spoke to Diana.

What followed had to be the worst evening Ryan had ever spent, and she had had a few of them since coming to Montgomery Hall three weeks ago.

Three weeks ... It didn't seem possible that so much had happened to her in that time. She had set out on that Saturday morning, in complete ignorance of the traumatic love that awaited her, thinking she was just going to spend three peaceful, uneventful weeks painting. As it turned out, she had done very little painting, only one completed canvas, and even that was still up in the studio. She felt loath to ask for its return.

'I'll go and get it,' Mark suggested after dinner, which had been a rather strained affair, with Grant being charming to Diana, the charm completely disappearing when he had, through necessity, to speak to Ryan. 'Like to come and see the studio, Diana?' he suggested softly.

'Oh, but——'

'I'd love to.' Diana ignored Ryan's plea, following Mark out of the room.

Ryan looked at Grant beneath lowered lashes, having the distinct feeling that Mark and Diana had deliberately left them alone like this. She had no idea what they hoped to achieve, but she could see Grant welcomed this time alone no more than she did.

The silence between them stretched on awkwardly, and Ryan kept shooting pleading glances in the direction of the door, longing for Mark and Diana's return.

'I have a feeling they think they're playing Cupid,' Grant drawled.

So did she—and she could have knocked their heads together! She and Grant had nothing to say to each other, she doubted they ever had.

'Unless Mark is just trying to get rid of you,' he added insultingly. 'It must be obvious to even the most casual of observers, and you're far from being that, that those two are in love.'

And Grant was far from being a casual observer too! He had been watching them all with the eyes of a hawk, seemed to know their every emotion.

'Well?' he rasped at her silence. 'Don't you have anything to say about them?'

She wetted her lips with the tip of her tongue. 'Congratulations?' She couldn't go on pretending to be in ignorance of Mark and Diana's love for each other any more.

'Is that all?'

'What else is there?' she shrugged.

'Nothing, obviously. You're taking this very well,' he frowned.

'Aren't I?' Her voice was brittle.

'Ryan—— Damn!' Grant swore as the telephone began to ring, snatching up the receiver.

Ryan tried not to listen, but as soon as she knew the late-night call was from Don Short she couldn't help but do so.

'Again?' Grant rasped, glancing at Ryan. 'But I thought he'd been kept away from them—— No, of course I'm not blaming you,' he sighed. 'You know what we have to do? Yes,' he acknowledged heavily, 'I'll tell her. It's my responsibility too. I'll be with you in about fifteen minutes.' He rang off with a worried frown.

For Ryan, even though she could only hear Grant's side, the conversation was only too lucid. 'You won't tell me anything!' she spoke fiercely to Grant's back, glaring at him as he slowly turned to face her, a frown between his deep green eyes. 'Ragtag and I are leaving here tomorrow, after that he'll never bother you again.'

'What are you talking about?' He seemed pre-occupied, dragging his attention back to her with effort. 'Who won't bother me?'

'I know, Grant,' she said heavily. 'I know who's killing the sheep. And I won't let you kill him.'

'It may have to be done——'

'Not if I take him away——'

'How can you take him away?' he snapped his impatience. 'For heaven's sake, Ryan, I don't have the time for this right now.'

'No,' her eyes glittered, 'you want to go out there and kill Ragtag,' her voice cracked. 'Well, I'm not going to let you. Once we're away from here——'

'You think I bought you Ragtag just to have him destroyed?' Grant's voice was icily dangerous.

Ryan looked at him closely, seeing the glowering anger in his eyes, the white fury about his mouth, and in that moment she knew she had been wrong about him, that there was no ruthless side to Grant, that he didn't want to hurt her.

Closely following her ecstatic relief came the agony of realising that he knew how she had misjudged him now, knew and was disgusted with her.

'Grant——'

'That's what you thought,' he ground out. '*That's* the reason you changed towards me. You made love with me, somehow gained the impression that it was your dog doing all the damage——'

'He isn't, is he?'

'No,' Grant rasped harshly, 'he isn't. But you thought I intended having him put down. *That's* the compensation you were offering!'

'I overheard you talking with Peter——'

'And broke your ankle on the strength of it.' His mouth twisted with open disgust now. 'What sort of man do you think I am, to make love to you one minute and then contemplate killing something you love so deeply the next? Don't bother to answer that,' he snapped. 'You obviously think I'm totally inhuman——'

'Grant, please——'

'Please!' he glared down at her. 'You dare to say please to me after thinking I'm some sort of emotionless monster! And all that rubbish you told me about an affair once you marry Mark—you didn't mean that, did you? You knew I'd never accept such an arrangement, *counted* on my not accepting.'

'Yes,' she admitted huskily.

'I don't have the time to waste here now,' he said impatiently. 'And you'll probably be gone by the time I do have this situation sorted out——'

'Grant——'

'There's no more to be said, Ryan,' he dismissed scathingly. 'Let's just chalk this one down to experience.'

'But I'm not——' she broke off, biting her bottom lip in consternation.

'Not experienced? No,' he sighed, 'I know you aren't, and that puzzled me. But I was willing to accept that you wished our lovemaking hadn't happened, that you do truly love Mark. But you don't, do you?'

'No.'

'Then why the hell—— No, never mind,' he ground out. 'That's probably something else I don't want to hear. Goodbye, Ryan. It's been a strange, if interesting, time, meeting you. I hope sincerely it's never repeated!' He stormed out of the room, the front door slamming a few seconds later.

Ryan was ashen. She had ruined everything with her mistrust, should have talked to Grant about her fears; the closeness they had achieved that night should have made that possible. Instead she had chosen to believe the worst, had judged him without a trial, and he would never forgive her for it.

'Ryan?' Mark was frowning as he came into the room. 'Was that Grant I heard leaving?'

'Yes, he—I——' and Ryan burst into tears, sobbing as if her heart would break.

She still felt terrible the next morning, knowing she had to see Grant just once more, if only to apologise. If he would let her apologise, that was! She couldn't blame him if he never wanted to see her again.

She had been too distraught to reveal the whole of her unfairness to Mark and Diana last night, had been too upset to talk coherently. They had seemed to respect her wish to be alone once they reached the cottage, and despite Diana's attempts to get her to confide this morning she had been met with a polite if friendly refusal. It was enough that she and Grant knew the extent of her stupidity.

'Ready?' Mark asked cheerfully when he arrived at the cottage just after ten.

'Ryan would like to go up to the Hall,' Diana told him quietly.

He frowned. 'I thought you said goodbye to Mandy? She said something about coming to stay with you in the summer.'

'She is,' Diana nodded, having become very good friends with Mandy too.

'Then why——'

'Don't be obtuse, Mark,' his girl-friend sighed as

Ryan became more and more embarrassed.

'But I don't—— Ah,' he grimaced, shaking his head as he saw Ryan's red face, 'I don't think now is a good time to see Grant.'

She looked at him with huge blue eyes. 'Why not?'

'He—— It just isn't a good idea.'

'Mark?' she frowned at his evasion. 'What is it? Has anything happened to him?' concern sharpened her voice.

'No.'

'Then what is it?' she demanded. 'And don't tell me nothing, I know you too well for that.'

'Okay,' he sighed. 'If you have to know . . .'

'I do.'

'Sam Clarke, one of our neighbours, shot Rex last night.'

She went suddenly pale. 'Rex?' she swallowed hard. 'Is he . . .?'

'Yes,' Mark nodded. 'Instantly.'

She couldn't believe that the beautiful Golden Labrador was dead. Not that she had had a lot to do with the two Labradors, but nevertheless, the thought of such a lovely creature dying so cruelly made her feel sick. And poor Grant, he had loved the dogs very deeply.

'Rex was the sheep-worrier,' Mark explained. 'It wasn't quite so bad when it was just our stock, but when he started on the neighbours' Grant knew he had to do something.'

'Last week,' Ryan realised numbly.

'Yes,' Mark gave her a puzzled frown, but he didn't pursue the subject of how she had known that. 'Your accident put things back a bit, and I think that all the time Grant was just hoping it would work out. He was thinking of arranging for Rex to be taken in by a town family when this last incident happened, although of course it had to be Mandy's final decision.'

'Mandy?'

He nodded. 'Rex was her dog, and Riba mine, but you know what it's like when you're younger, you get sidetracked, and dogs become the last thing on your mind,' he gave Diana a pointed look. 'It just seemed natural that Grant should take charge of them both, he and Don. That was partly the reason it took them so long to realise it was Rex—Grant would think he was with Don, Don would think he was with Grant, and all the time he was with the sheep.' He shrugged. 'Maybe it's as well it worked out this way. I doubt Rex would have liked town life, and Mandy would have hated Grant if he had to put Rex down.'

As she had done! Poor Grant, how he must despise her. And poor Rex; he had been such a lovely dog.

'I'd still like to see Grant, if you don't mind,' she said quietly, knowing it would be her last chance to tell him how very sorry she was.

'I don't mind,' Mark shrugged. 'But he really isn't in the best of humours.'

'I'll risk it.'

Mandy was in the drawing-room when they arrived at the Hall, her eyes red-rimmed from crying. Ryan felt for her, knowing how she had felt when she thought it was to be Ragtag who died.

'Grant's in his study,' the other girl informed her.

Ryan nodded. 'I won't be long.'

She felt as nervous as the day she had arrived here as she stood outside Grant's study, more nervous if she thought of the degree of intimacy she had attained with Grant since that time. If only they could go back to that night together, with no interruption from Don, no overheard conversation with Peter, no stupid accident. How different things could have been between them in the morning when they woke in each other's arms—how wonderfully different.

Before she had a chance to knock, while her expression still showed the memory of Grant's lovemaking, the study door was flung open and Grant's eyes narrowed as he looked down at her.

His head rose haughtily, his nostrils flaring. 'I thought you'd be long gone,' he rasped. 'Mark left over an hour ago.'

Not an auspicious beginning! 'I—er—I came to say goodbye,' her voice came out as a husky squeak.

His expression became even more remote. 'I thought we did that last night.'

'I—— No, *you* said goodbye, I didn't.'

Grant gave an impatient sigh, the hardness of his mouth unyielding as he walked back to sit behind the desk. 'You'd better come in,' he snapped as she hovered in the doorway.

Ryan went inside and closed the door, but she felt tongue-tied as Grant glowered at her across the desk. 'I just—I want to apologise,' she looked at him pleadingly.

He gave a haughty inclination of his head, obviously in no mood to sympathise with her stupidity.

'And I'm so sorry about Rex.' Her voice broke emotionally. Grant's eyes showed pain for a brief moment, then he was under control once again. 'We all are,' he said distantly.

She hadn't expected that he would make this easy for her, and she wasn't disappointed. How she longed to erase the frown from between his eyes, the lines of bitterness grooved into his cheeks, the cynical twist to his mouth. And she had denied herself the right to even touch him.

'I'm sorry for what I said to you, *thought* about you.'

A strange expression flickered across his face, but before she could analyse it it had gone, the dark green depths of his eyes once again cold. 'We all make mistakes,' he dismissed.

Ryan swallowed hard. 'As you did—about me?'

'Exactly,' he gave an abrupt nod of his head.

She felt the tears well into her eyes. She had never felt so—so helpless as she did at that moment. This was the man she loved, the man she belonged to heart and soul, and he didn't want her.

'Mark tells me you had a visit from Valerie yesterday,' he said suddenly.

Darn Mark! 'Yes,' she confirmed.

'I feel sure it wasn't a social call,' he said dryly. 'I'm sorry if she upset you at all.'

'She—she said the two of you were going to be married.'

Icy green eyes raked over her. 'Did she?'

'Is—is it true?'

He looked irritated by the question. 'I don't think you have any right to ask that question. Any plans I have for marriage do not concern you.'

'No, I—No, they don't. I'm sorry. Goodbye.' Ryan turned too suddenly on her crutches, and as she felt the support go on her right side, she called out Grant's name as she toppled over.

'For heaven's sake——!' Grant somehow managed to stop her actually hitting the carpeted floor, pulling her hard against him. 'Are you all right?' he murmured against her lips.

'I'm very all right now. Oh, Grant, kiss me!' she begged him, her mouth raised invitingly.

'Ryan——!'

'Please, Grant!' She touched the hardness of his cheek with loving fingers.

'Why not?' he said hardly, and his mouth lowered on hers to force her lips apart.

She wanted gentleness from him, the tender emotion she had from him the night they had made love so beautifully. Instead his lips were hard and demanding on hers, no trace of desire in the ruthless assault of his mouth on hers, only a desire to punish, to hurt as he had been hurt.

'No!' She wrenched away from him, looking up at him with bewildered eyes.

'Not what you wanted?' His mouth twisted with contempt as he released her. 'But this is hardly the time or place for that, Ryan. Maybe if you ever come back on a visit with Mark,' he drawled insultingly.

'Grant . . .?'

He raised dark brows. 'What happened to the liberated girl who so easily dismissed what we had together only a few days ago?' he taunted.

She swallowed hard, pain in her deep blue depths. 'You know I'm not liberated——'

'Yes,' he bit out. 'And I still have to work out why I was given the privilege of being your first lover.'

Ryan flinched as if he had physically struck her. 'It isn't too difficult to work out if you think about it,' she said dully.

'Maybe I don't care to,' he dismissed coldly.

She bit her top lip, taking one last look at the man she loved. 'If you ever—do,' she told him huskily, 'Mark knows where I live.'

Grant nodded abruptly. 'I'll bear it in mind. Who knows, maybe I could—call on you,' he drawled, 'when I go to the gallery next time.'

'I—Yes,' she held back her tears, 'Of course. I— Goodbye, then.'

'Goodbye, Ryan,' he nodded abruptly.

CHAPTER TEN

WITHIN weeks Ryan had her plaster removed from her ankle, and returned to college, hoping to bury her pain in her absorption in her work. It didn't turn out that way. London no longer held her enthralled, seemed too big and noisy, the parties too wild, with everyone wanting to enjoy themselves too badly.

When she allowed herself the luxury of thought she longed for the wide open peace of the Yorkshire hills, for those long tranquil walks amongst the heather and gorse, but most of all she longed for a green-eyed devil to melt her bones to water.

She knew Grant must have been up to his gallery in London at least twice in the last two months, and she had even called at the gallery herself, feeling close to him there, but he had made no effort to come and see her, and she told herself he never would.

She heard nothing of him from Mark and Diana, both of them seeming to steer clear of talking about him, and she was too afraid to broach the subject of him herself, fearing what she might hear about him and Valerie.

Grant hadn't denied intending to marry Valerie when she had asked him. Oh, how she wished she could have been his bride!

But if he was back with Valerie neither Mark nor Diana told her about it, although just lately the two of them seemed to be more deeply involved than ever. Ryan was happy for them, although she would be a liar if she didn't admit to feeling envious of them too.

She had turned down all offers of dates since she had been back in London, compared every man she met to Grant—and knew that they all fell far short of the magnetically attractive man he was and always would be.

But she was feeling particularly miserable this Friday afternoon in June. Mark and Diana were leaving for Montgomery Hall straight after college, and the weekend stretched in front of her long and lonely.

'Ryan!'

She turned at the sound of that light, familiar voice, feeling none of the heart-stopping excitement that had overtaken her whenever Alan used to look at her like this. Now she saw him for what he was, a man who would be a perennial student, a man still boyish and reckless, a man who would never grow up and accept the responsibilities of life, least of all those of loving someone. She could see that now, and felt nothing towards him but a warm friendship.

'Alan!' she smiled as she waited for him to catch up with her in the corridor where he taught and she was taught.

'On your way to class?'

She grimaced, nodding. 'But my heart isn't in it.'

His blue eyes lightened. His blond hair was longer than was fashionable, and his tight denims and loose tee-shirt gave him no distinction from his students. 'Shall we give it a miss this afternoon, like we used to?' His voice had lowered seductively.

Ryan blushed as she remembered how they had spent those afternoons of truancy. 'Not today, Alan,' she refused distantly. 'I missed a few classes while my ankle was bad.'

He looked down. 'How is it now?'

'Fine.' And it was. Only her heart remained broken from her visit to Sleaton.

'And am I forgiven?'

She frowned. Forgiven...? 'I—Oh yes,' she blushed anew, having forgotten how they parted, the reason they had parted. She could never have loved this man if she had baulked at a physical relationship with him, she had not given it a second thought when Grant had wanted her. 'Of course,' she told him awkwardly.

'Feel like sharing a bottle of wine with me tonight?'

Her refusal hovered on her lips. But why not? Why not spend a harmless evening with him? It would mean she wouldn't be alone, and there was no danger of it being more than he offered, a simple sharing of a bottle of wine.

She smiled. 'You'll bring the wine?'

'And you'll supply the scintillating company?'

'I'll try,' she laughed.

'Good. I'll see you about eight.' Alan bent and kissed her briefly on the mouth, a look of triumph in his eyes as he went on his way to his next class.

It was that gleam of triumph that bothered Ryan the rest of the afternoon, a nagging doubt that persisted even though she told herself it was only a chat and a glass of wine.

Diana was bustling about preparing for her weekend away when Ryan got home, and she emerged breathlessly from the bathroom towelling her hair dry. 'Dinner's in the oven,' she hurried into the bedroom to dress.

Ryan gave a shrug of acceptance and went to eat her solitary dinner, clearing away when Diana emerged from the bedroom looking like someone who had been transformed into a butterfly, glowingly beautiful.

'Do I look all right?' she asked nervously.

'Of course,' Ryan frowned, never having seen Diana look lovelier. 'Special occasion?'

Diana blushed coyly. 'We intend telling Grant this weekend that we're going to be married.'

'That's marvellous!' Ryan's enthusiastic approval was warm and excited; she hugged Diana, treating Mark to the same when he arrived a few minutes later.

Her pleasure fell very flat once the other couple had left, and she really couldn't get up any enthusiasm for her date with Alan. How would Grant take the news of the engagement? She felt sure he liked Diana, and it was a certainty that Diana would make Mark a better wife than she ever would. Together she and Mark would have had no stability at all.

Alan kissed her lightly on the lips again when he arrived shortly after eight, although he seemed quite happy to sit and chat for the next couple of hours, their mutual interest in art giving them ample scope for conversation.

But nevertheless, Ryan couldn't help but compare him with Grant—unfavourably. It was like comparing cologne to Chanel No. 5, plonk to champagne. There was no comparison!

'Where have you gone to?' Fingers clicked in front of her unseeing eyes as Alan came to sit beside her on the sofa.

She blinked back to an awareness of her surroundings, remembering other evenings they had spent in this way, relaxed in casual denims and tee-shirts, sipping wine, munching on crisps and peanuts, Alan smoking a constant stream of cigarettes, something that Ryan found she no longer liked. She never used to mind the clinging smell of the smoke, having to open all the windows wide to air the room out, but now she resented his assumption that it was all right to stink her home out with those strong cigarettes he favoured.

'Ryan?' he frowned.

Ryan swallowed hard, knowing it had been a mistake to let him come here tonight. She had wanted company, but this was the wrong face, the wrong *man*.

'I have a headache,' she invented, standing up restlessly. 'I think I should get to bed.'

'Ryan . . .?'

'Not with you!' she snapped her irritation with the hopeful look on his face. 'I haven't changed in that respect.'

He shrugged. 'One can always hope.'

'Not where I'm concerned,' she flashed.

'But I thought——'

'Yes, what did you think?' she frowned. 'That because I accepted your invitation to spend the evening with you I'd also accepted going to bed with you? I thought you knew me better than that, Alan.' He flushed his anger, and she knew she had been right. 'I think you'd better go,' she said wearily.

'I wanted us to be friends——'

'So did I,' she glared at him. '*Just* friends.'

Alan put his wine glass down and stood up. 'You're a damned prude,' he scorned. 'No girl of twenty-one is a virgin nowadays.'

'Who said I was?' Ryan was very angry herself now. 'Maybe I'm just a little more discriminating than you about who I go to bed *with*.'

It had been the wrong thing to say, she could see that as soon as the words had left her mouth. Alan's eyes glittered with fury, his mouth tightening as he made a lunge towards her.

'And maybe you're just a little tease,' he ground out, his hands painful on her arms. 'Maybe what you really need is a little force!' His mouth came down painfully on hers.

Ryan had never realised how strong he was, that his wiry body hid a ripcord strength she couldn't even begin to fight, although she tried, hating his mouth on hers, his hands exploring her body in fevered caresses, that he might be deriving enjoyment from but which only sickened her.

But suddenly he was pushing away from her. 'What the hell——!' He turned angrily, looking down to where Ragtag was pulling on his trouser leg, growling low in his throat as he shook the material. 'Get this damned animal off me!' he shouted angrily, trying to shake loose of the clamped teeth.

Ryan didn't know whether to laugh or be angry. Since they had been in London Ragtag had seemed completely cured of his aversion to men, although he definitely didn't like Alan. He was right not to. Alan's intent was obvious, and where charm had failed he intended force to succeed. Ragtag had other ideas.

'Let go, Ragtag!' she instructed, holding his collar to pull him away, looking challengingly at Alan as he bent to inspect his trousers.

'He's ripped the damned material!' he snapped, glaring at the unrepentant dog.

'Yes,' Ryan nodded, as Ragtag stayed at her side.

'Well, don't sound so damned happy about it!'

She sighed. 'I'm not happy about it, although I'd prefer your denims to be ripped to being raped myself.'

Dull colour entered his cheeks. 'I wouldn't have raped you.'

'You would have had to,' she told him quietly.

'Why?' he asked exasperatedly. 'I always thought you were attracted to me.'

'I was.'

'Was?' Alan echoed sharply.

Ryan nodded. 'I think you'd better leave.'

'No, I——' he broke off as the dog at her side began to growl again. 'Why don't you put him in the bedroom and we can talk? he said persuasively.

'Talk?' She raised her eyebrows mockingly.

He flushed. 'What's the matter with you, Ryan?' he demanded irritably. 'What's wrong with going to bed with someone?'

'Nothing,' she smiled at this new ploy. 'As long as you want to go to bed with that someone. I don't happen to want to go to bed with you. And there's nothing wrong with me, so don't think I'll meet that challenge.'

He picked up his jacket with a disgruntled scowl. 'I might as well go, then. I have better things to do than waste my time with a little tease.'

Ryan allowed him his moment of anger, taking the wine glasses and bottle through to the kitchen as she heard him leave. So much for a harmless evening!

'An angry man at the door just told me I was taking my life into my hands coming in here to face the vicious animal. I hope he meant Ragtag!'

Ryan had spun round at the first sound of that achingly familiar voice, the glass slipping out of her hand as she gazed at Grant with shocked eyes.

'Careful!' he ordered as she almost stepped on to the broken glass with her bare feet, having moved towards him without realising it. 'We don't want any more accidents.' He went down on his haunches to pick up the biggest pieces of glass, putting them in the bin. 'Do you have a dustpan and brush? No, don't move,' he instructed firmly. 'Just tell me where it is.'

'I—In the cupboard, over there,' she pointed behind him.

This couldn't really be happening, Grant couldn't

really be here, and he certainly couldn't be crouched at her feet sweeping up broken glass. She must be hallucinating, must have drunk more wine than she had realised.

But if it was an hallucination it was a very good one. Grant's dark hair was thick and springy, and her fingers ached to touch it; his face was as strong and handsome as she remembered, the pale green shirt and dark green trousers he wore showing the leashed strength of his body as he stood up to dispose of the glass and put the dustpan and brush back in the cupboard.

Lean fingers closed about her upper arms as he moved her to one side, turning on the taps to rinse his hands under the hot water. 'Sticky,' he grimaced. 'What was in the glass?'

'Wine,' she croaked, wondering at the fact that she could talk at all. This wasn't an hallucination! Hallucinations didn't do practical things like sweep up broken glass and wash their hands.

Grant was really here! But *what* was he doing here? It was ten-thirty at night, hardly the time to make a social call. Besides, he should be at the Hall with Mark and Diana.

He had dried his hands now, and was looking at her through narrowed lids. 'You didn't answer my question,' he prompted.

'What question?' Ryan asked dazedly, mesmerised at his presence here, hardly daring to question why he was here.

'Are you the vicious animal?' His mouth quirked.

His humour broke the spell, and she gave a breathless laugh. 'No, that's Ragtag.'

'This Ragtag?' He bent down to stroke the dog roughly, Ragtag loving every minute of it. 'He wouldn't hurt anyone.' Grant straightened, while adoring brown eyes looked up at him.

He certainly wouldn't hurt Grant, he was behaving like a lovesick idiot over him! Or perhaps Grant just brought back happy memories of Sleaton; Ryan knew Ragtag hadn't been very happy in London.

'It depends who it is,' she shrugged. 'He didn't take too kindly to Alan being here.'

'The man who just left?'

'Yes.'

'And did you?' Grant prompted softly.

'Not really,' she shook her head. 'It was a mistake. We used to be—close, but not any more.'

'No?'

'No,' she said briskly. 'Shall we move out of the kitchen?' she suggested nervously. 'It's much more comfortable in the lounge.'

Grant preceded her through to the adjoining room. 'It's a comfortable flat. What will you do when Diana moves out?' He turned to look at her.

She swallowed hard. 'They told you they're getting married?'

His mouth hardened. 'Amongst other things.'

Ryan stiffened, but the hardness of Grant's face told her nothing. 'Other things . . .?' she repeated lightly.

'Yes. Tell me, how do you like being back in London?'

She found his evasion annoying. What else had Mark told him? Had they mentioned her at all, or did Grant still believe she had wanted to marry Mark?

'I—It's home,' she shrugged.

'Is it?'

She frowned. 'I—Yes.'

Grant stretched his long length out in one of the armchairs. 'I've always believed in that old cliché that home is where the heart is.'

'Yes?' Ryan was wary now.

'Yes.' Cool green eyes held her mesmerised, the blandness of his expression telling her nothing that he didn't want her to know. 'Don't you believe that too?' he quirked his dark brows.

She ran the tip of her tongue lightly along the edge of her mouth, an unconsciously provocative gesture that darkened the colour of Grant's eyes, then blushed as she realised his gaze was fixed on the slow caressing movement. 'I—I've never thought about it,' she said jerkily.

Grant was very relaxed, like a sleek jungle cat, with the ability to pounce if it became necessary. And she was the only 'victim' in sight! 'I've been thinking of a lot of things the last two months, even more intensely on the drive down here this evening. I must admit that—Alan, came as something of a surprise to me, Diana assured me you'd been seeing no one since you came back to London.'

Ryan flushed. 'Why should she tell you something like that?'

'Because I asked her,' he said with cool arrogance. 'Those thoughts I'd been having only needed slight verification.'

His calmness, his relaxation when she was a bundle of nerves, made her reply short and angry. 'What were these thoughts?' she snapped.

His gaze roamed slowly over her flushed face. 'Loyalty and friendship are special qualities,' he said slowly.

'Yes.'

'Will you give me the same loyalty and friendship you gave to Mark?'

Friendship? He wanted *friendship* from her? She looked at him with bewildered eyes. She couldn't accept friendship from him, wanted more, so very much more——

'And love, of course,' he added softly. 'The same love you gave me on the most memorably beautiful night of my life.'

'Grant . . .?' she gasped.

He was standing now, coming towards her, the most incredibly *loving* expression on his face. 'I told you I didn't care to think about your reasons for that night,' he murmured softly, his eyes full of tenderness, his mouth gentle as he kissed her brow, holding her lightly in his arms. 'After you'd gone I could think of nothing else,' he shuddered at the memory, his face buried in her hair. 'I thought of your beauty, your gentleness, your love for anything hurt or in trouble, of the way you give love unreservedly, and I knew that that night you gave *me* love. You did, didn't you, Ryan?'

'Yes.' She quivered in his arms, afraid to believe he could be here to tell her he felt the same way. He couldn't be here for that—maybe he was just an hallucination after all? If he was it could go on for a lifetime!

'You love me?' Grant spoke huskily against her throat.

She trembled as his lips probed her skin. 'Yes.'

'And I love you, did you know that?'

Ryan looked up at him, afraid to believe what she was hearing. 'Say—say that again.'

His smile was gentle, his lips caressing against hers. 'I love you, Ryan. I've loved you from the beginning, I think.'

'No——'

'Yes.' His mouth roamed the silkiness of her face, mounting desire within her, each nerve, each particle of her being attuned to his caress. 'Can we talk later, darling?' he moaned huskily against her lips. 'Right now I need to convince myself—and you—that we love each other, that once the explanations have been made we're going to be married.'

'Married?' Ryan swallowed hard, her trembling hands groping on to his shirt front as she searched his love-softened features for the truth of his words.

'Yes—married, my darling,' he smiled down at her. 'I'm going to tie you to me for ever, never out of my sight or my heart for the rest of our lives. Now, do I have your permission to convince you with more than words?' he teased gently.

Her eyes glowed as she slowly nodded her head, and as his mouth claimed hers her lips parted to deepen the kiss, her whole body shaking as she allowed herself to believe in heaven, heaven here on earth, in Grant's arms . . .

A long time later they lay in each other's arms, Grant lying back on the sofa, Ryan nestled against his bare chest, his heartbeat at last beginning to steady, the rapid rise and fall of his chest starting to regulate.

'I didn't think it could possibly be as good as the first time,' his voice was gruff, 'but it was better! Oh, my darling . . .!' he kissed her heatedly, turning to press her back into the cushions, desire at once rekindling. 'I could make love to you all night,' he groaned. 'In fact,' he raised his head to smile, 'I intend to.'

Ryan buried her face against his chest, amazed she could still feel this way after the intimacies they had once again shared.

'Don't be shy,' he raised her chin gently. 'You believe I love you?' he frowned.

'Oh yes!' Her eyes glowed, leaving him in no doubt as to his feelings for her. He had told her time and time again as he made love to her, had left her in no doubt of his love. 'And I love you.'

His eyes deepened in colour. 'That first day I met you I had no idea how important one tiny young lady was going to be in my life.'

'Tiny?' She pretended indignation.

Grant looked down at her nakedness, his eyes darkening as he cupped one creamy breast. 'Perfect,' he kissed the taut nipple. 'I can't wait for the day I see my child taking its life force from this exact spot,' and his lips caressed the nipple once more.

Delicate colour heightened her cheeks. She wanted Grant's child too, and the thought of it filled her with delicious wonder. 'We were talking about the day you met the tiny young lady you love,' she prompted to cover her emotion.

'Coward!' he laughed softly. 'Yes,' he sighed, 'I had no idea when I first looked into a pair of stormy blue eyes that within a very short time, a matter of days, in fact, you would be the woman I love. Before we go any further,' he frowned, 'I think I should explain Valerie. No, don't,' he pleaded as she would have moved away. 'I went out with her, I'll admit I even went to bed with her, but I never loved her, and I never told her I did.'

'She seemed to think she was going to be your wife,' Ryan said huskily.

'Never,' Grant said fiercely. 'It was never even a possibility. I was far from being Valerie's first lover, Ryan, and I very much doubt I'll be the last. The Valeries of this world needn't bother you, darling. Don't you know you're the very pinnacle of my existence, the reason I want to live for a thousand years?'

'I'm that—important to you?'

'More.' His arms tightened about her. 'You mean more to me than anything else in my life ever has— more than the estate, more than Mandy or Mark.'

'I'm not just another one of your orphaned lambs you like to take in and care for?'

He laughed softly. 'You certainly aren't a lamb, more like a lioness, and I'd want to marry you even if I had to fight parents and six brothers to get you. And talking of brothers, how could you let me believe you were in love with Mark?'

Ryan blushed guiltily. 'At the start it didn't really pose a problem, but later——'

'When you fell in love with me,' said Grant with satisfaction.

'Yes,' she smiled. 'Then it was a problem.'

'Don't I know it!' he grimaced. 'The night we made love, I tried to stop, to tell myself you belonged to Mark, but it didn't matter. I wanted you, loved you, and I had to have you. I knew you were an innocent, and when you denied it I couldn't understand why. Then I thought that perhaps you regretted it, that *you* thought that if I knew it had been your important first time I might tell Mark and ruin things for you with him. When he told me tonight that he was going to marry Diana I didn't know whether to throttle him for hurting you or thank him for leaving you free. I finally did the former, although I didn't quite throttle him. Then he explained everything,' Grant's expression was stern. 'And that's where your loyalty and friendship came in, wasn't it, even over your love for me?'

'Yes.' Ryan was so relieved he knew, so relieved it was over.

'Mark had no need to go to those lengths, you know.

Oh, I might have been—overprotective—in the past, but I knew straight away that Diana would make him the steadying, loving wife that he needs. You, however, were a different matter.'

She touched the dark wiry hair on his chest, feeling how his skin had cooled after their lovemaking, her lips tasting salty after she had bent and kissed the hardness of his flat stomach.

'Don't try and change the subject!' He pretended disapproval, spoiling the effect with his fierce kiss. 'You would never have been a good wife for Mark, you're too independent, too fiery, too——'

'—Much in love with you,' she finished huskily.

'Yes!' he laughed triumphantly, then suddenly sobered. 'I have some other news for you, if you're interested, about Mandy.' He raised dark brows.

There was only one thing Ryan wanted to hear about Mandy, and from Grant's air of indulgence she had a feeling he had given up on the idea of his sister marrying Colin. 'She's going to marry Peter,' she said excitedly.

He frowned. 'How did you know that? No, don't tell me,' he sighed. 'You seem to have been their confidante over the last few months. I can't understand where I went wrong,' he shook his head.

Ryan smoothed the frown from between his eyes. 'You didn't go wrong, darling, Mark and Mandy just grew up without your realising it. They have Diana and Peter to depend on now——'

'And you have me.'

She nodded. 'And I'll never lie to you or hold anything back from you. I only want to make you happy.'

That deserved renewed kisses and caresses, and it was several minutes before either of them felt the need for speech.

'Diana said she'll stay at the Hall until we get back,' Grant murmured into her throat. 'I think we should stay here long enough to get married. The end of the week should do it.'

Ryan had no objection to that; she would have married him tomorrow if it could have been arranged. 'You haven't told me yet how Mandy and Peter sorted out their troubles,' she pouted.

'You romantic!' Grant teased softly.

'Well, they seemed so—apart.'

'They were.' He sobered. 'And that was my fault too—although I had no idea of that, I didn't even know they were in love. You see, ten years ago, I was engaged——'

'To Rebecca—I know.'

He gave a rueful smile. 'I should have known. Mandy, right?'

'Yes,' she admitted huskily. 'She said you loved Rebecca very much.'

'I did—in a calf-love sort of way.' He grimaced. 'I knew just after we got engaged that I'd made a mistake, but it seemed too late then to do anything about it, Rebecca was already arranging the wedding. Then she and Peter came to me and said they'd fallen in love, that she wanted to end the engagement. Of course I said yes, but before anything could be done about announcing the broken engagement Rebecca was killed in a car crash. By then it was superfluous to tell people I'd no longer been in love with her, and I had cared for her. All this time Peter has been feeling guilty about what happened, and when he fell in love with Mandy he decided to fight it—he didn't think it fair that he now wanted to marry my sister. I drove her over to his house on the way over here once I knew she loved him, and they should have worked it all out by now. It only remains for us to reunite Ragtag with his loved one, and then everyone will be happy.'

'Ragtag?' Ryan repeated incredulously. 'I don't understand.'

Grant grinned. 'At the beginning of the week Riba presented him with six progeny, two boys and four girls.'

'Ragtag and *Riba*?' she gasped.

'Yes,' he laughed. 'They couldn't be anyone else's but Ragtag's, they're the cutest puppies I've ever seen.'

She could imagine they were. 'But don't you mind?' she frowned.

'No,' he smiled.

Now she had her answer as to where Ragtag kept disappearing—he had a girl-friend of his own! 'I can't believe it!' she laughed happily.

'I'm not quite sure Riba does yet.' Grant sobered. 'I think I owe you an apology, darling.'

'Apology?'

'On the day you arrived I was very derogatory about your art. I have to confess to taking a look at your work in the studio—and I just want you to know that I shall be very proud to bring another great artist into the family.'

'Me?'

'You,' he nodded gravely. 'You have a rare and wonderful talent, my darling, one I intend you to nurture.'

Grant as a husband, Ragtag, that wonderful studio for all time—she didn't deserve such happiness. 'Is this a dream?' she asked dazedly.

'Definitely not.' He stood up with her in his arms. 'I need your warmth again, Ryan, the wonderful way you have of giving. I shall always need that, my darling.'

And she was convinced of that time and time again through the night of love they spent in each other's arms.

PORTRAIT OF A GREAT PAINTER

Anna Mary Robertson Moses' immensely successful career as an artist spanned twenty-two years. Her paintings, mostly of happy rural scenes, hang in major museums, and she has been acclaimed by critics and the public alike. This may not sound extraordinary—except that Anna did not begin to paint until she reached the age of seventy-eight!

Born in 1860, she grew up near the town of Greenwich in upstate New York. At twenty-seven she married Thomas Moses, and they settled on a farm and began to raise a family.

Thomas died in 1927, but Anna kept busy—running the farm, sewing and doing embroidery. As she grew older she developed painful arthritis, and her sister suggested she try painting as a pastime.

Her first pictures were copies of scenes depicted on Christmas cards, which Anna exhibited at country fairs. A visiting New York City antique dealer discovered her work in a local drugstore and introduced her to a gallery owner. Before long Anna had her first show: "What a Farm Wife Painted." A reporter called her Grandma Moses and the name stuck.

Mostly she painted "old-timey things," pictures Anna saw as dreams of the past. But in spite of her success, she was always first and foremost a down-to-earth farm wife. When she was entertained at the White House by President Truman, they didn't talk politics—"We talked plowin'."

On her ninetieth birthday Grandma Moses promised she would dance a jig on her hundredth, and she lived to keep that promise. Shortly before she died, at 101, she said, "I look back on my life as a good day's work. It was done and I feel satisfied."

A Harlequin

ROBERTA LEIGH

Collector's Edition

A specially designed collection of six exciting love stories by one of the world's favorite romance writers—Roberta Leigh, author of more than 60 bestselling novels!

1 Love in Store
2 Night of Love
3 Flower of the Desert

4 The Savage Aristocrat
5 The Facts of Love
6 Too Young to Love

Available now wherever paperback books are sold, or available through Harlequin Reader Service. Simply complete and mail the coupon below.

Harlequin Reader Service

In the U.S.
P.O. Box 52040
Phoenix, AZ 85072-9988

In Canada
649 Ontario Street
Stratford, Ontario N5A 6W2

Please send me the following editions of the Harlequin Roberta Leigh Collector's Editions. I am enclosing my check or money order for $1.95 for each copy ordered, plus 75¢ to cover postage and handling.

☑ 1　　☑ 2　　☑ 3　　☑ 4　　☑ 5　　☑ 6

Number of books checked ____6____ @ $1.95 each = $ _____

N.Y. state and Ariz. residents add appropriate sales tax	$	
Postage and handling	$	.75
TOTAL	$	

I enclose _____

(Please send check or money order. We cannot be responsible for cash sent through the mail.) Price subject to change without notice.

NAME _maria placido_

(Please Print)

ADDRESS _53 Wyndham St_　APT. NO. _53_

CITY _Toronto Ontario_

STATE/PROV. ___ ZIP/POSTAL CODE _M6K-1Z9_

Offer expires February 29, 1984

RL-N

30856000000

Get this book FREE!

Harlequin American Romance

Twice in a Lifetime
REBECCA FLANDERS

Mail to:
Harlequin Reader Service

In the U.S.
2504 West Southern Avenue
Tempe, AZ 85282

In Canada
649 Ontario Street
Stratford, Ontario N5A 6W2

YES! I want to be one of the first to discover
Harlequin American Romance. Send me FREE and without
obligation *Twice in a Lifetime.* If you do not hear from me after I
have examined my FREE book, please send me the 4 new
Harlequin American Romances each month as soon as they
come off the presses. I understand that I will be billed only $2.25
for each book (total $9.00). There are no shipping or handling
charges. There is no minimum number of books that I have to
purchase. In fact, I may cancel this arrangement at any time.
Twice in a Lifetime is mine to keep as a FREE gift, even if I do not
buy any additional books.

Name _____ (please print)

Address _____ Apt. no.

City _____ State/Prov. _____ Zip/Postal Code

Signature (If under 18, parent or guardian must sign.)

AR-SUB-300